Lock Down Publications and Ca$h
Presents

STEPPERS

Written By
KING RIO

First Edition 2023

Printed in the United States of America

Lock Down Publications
P.O. Box 944
Stockbridge, GA 30281
www.lockdownpublications.com

Like our page on Facebook: Lock Down Publications
www.facebook.com/lockdownpublications.ldp

Stay Connected with Us!

Text **LOCKDOWN** to 22828 to stay up-to-date with new releases, sneak peaks, contests and more…

Like our page on Facebook:
Lock Down Publications

Join Lock Down Publications/The New Era Reading Group

Visit our website:
www.lockdownpublications.com

Follow us on Instagram:
Lock Down Publications

Email Us: We want to hear from you!

Prologue
Terror in the Workplace

Thirty-year old CEO Johnna Broward stood at the curb in front of Panteon Technologies with her small, brown hands balled into fists at her sides. Her fingernails were stiletto-tipped, sharp like the claws of a lioness, and there was blood and flesh caked beneath the three remaining nails on her left hand. The left side of her bottom lip had a deep cut in it, and she kept using her tongue to probe the newly chipped canine tooth behind the bleeding laceration. Her nose was a little swollen. The left side of her head throbbed relentlessly.

The police were en route. Johnna could hear their sirens in the distance. On the sidewalk behind her, roughly half of Panteon's first-shift employees milled around with their phones to their ears and their eyes filled with tears. Security guard Romero Alvarez lay sprawled on his generous belly in front of the opaque glass doors just beyond the crowd. There was a bullet wound the size of a nickel below his right nostril and a ghastly exit wound at the back of his head that looked large enough to fit a softball in. Someone had been thoughtful enough to drape a headscarf over his cratered skull.

A small portion of Romero's brain was glued to the red bottom of Johnna's left shoe. She'd stepped on it as she ran from the building moments earlier. There were four more dead bodies inside the five-story, 48,000-square-foot office building. JaMika Lloyd, Tabitha Green, Anthony Ferguson, and Michael Caldwell.

Michael was the disgruntled, former employee who'd heartlessly gunned down the others. Romero had been the first to go, then Jamika at the front desk, and Tabby outside the elevator. Michael took to the fifth floor and finally Black Ant, the loyal assistant who had tried and failed to overtake Michael as he made his way toward Johnna's spacious, top-floor office.

Unarmed and deathly afraid, Johnna had sat frozen beneath her desk as Michael shot the lock off her office door and kicked it open. Trembling in fear, with her frightened hazel eyes agape and her knees drawn up to her chin, she'd watched his Nike running shoes as he walked around to the rear of her desk, and then, he'd reached under it and snatched her up by the throat with one powerful, Black hand.

"You know what the fuck I'm here for," he'd shouted in her face, and before she could reply, he backhanded her so hard that she went flailing across the room.

The side of her head struck the mahogany-paneled wall with enough force to knock her framed college degree askew. The impact had dazed her, and the next thing she knew, she was on all fours with blood pouring from her mouth. A fleeting image of her devilishly handsome older brother, Johnny "Bang Boy" Broward, had flashed across her mind's eye. Then, Michael's hand was on the back of her head, slamming her face into the plushy carpeted floor.

"You got five seconds to tell me where it's at, Johnna," he'd growled through clenched teeth. "Five. Fuckin'. *Seconds.*"

Lord God, Johnna remembered praying, *please forgive me of my sins. Give me a way out of this and I promise to make it up to You. And if it's not in Your will for me to live, then please watch over my family, give me my wings, and allow me into Your kingdom.*

And then, mere seconds later, she'd heard two thunderous cracks of gunfire. She'd squeezed her eyes shut and prepared herself for the afterlife, but when she opened her eyes, she was still face down on the blood-spotted, gray carpet, and when she looked over, she saw Michael laid out next to her, his eyes open and lifeless, a grisly exit wound in the middle of his forehead.

It was a good thing she'd hired a second security guard three days prior. His name was Jayvon Sullivan, and he'd arrived at her office just in time to save her life.

"You okay?" Jayvon had asked as he holstered his pistol and helped Johnna to her feet, and now, as he walked up beside her and placed an arm around her shoulders, he repeated the question.

Johnna nodded her head and said nothing. She snuggled up against him and wept in silence as the first NYPD patrol cars careened into the vast front parking lot and made a beeline toward the building. Johnna had always found comfort in the presence of a tall, Black man, and Jayvon was mild-mannered and giant, 6'6" and nearly three hundred pounds of solid muscle. Johnna was a strong-minded, Black woman, who, in her younger years, had been known to drag a bitch when disrespect came her way, but she was only 5'1". She looked like a child standing next to Jayvon.

A news chopper flew by overhead. Johnna looked up, squinting against the blinding sun, and saw the CNN logo on the side of the tail. It was a hot, late, spring day in lower Manhattan, the kind of day she'd usually spend with her sorority sisters, splashing about in the marble-lined swimming pool behind her fifty-million-dollar mansion in The Hamptons, but right now, all Johnna wanted to do was board her private jet and fly back to Chicago — not just because it was her hometown but also because she knew it was where she'd find the man who'd sent Michael Caldwell on a broad-day killing spree.

Chapter 1

Detective Richard McKenzie was an eleven-year veteran with the NYPD Red, the New York Police Department's clandestine division of detectives responsible for investigating crimes against the city's elite. And since Forbes had Johnna Broward's current net worth at $2.8 billion, making her the third-richest Black woman in America behind Alexus Costilla and Oprah, the mass shooting at Panteon Technologies had been assigned to McKenzie and his rookie partner, Erica Sinclair.

Sinclair researched Johnna Broward on her laptop while McKenzie maneuvered their SUV through Midtown Manhattan.

"Okay, here's what we have," said Sinclair. "Johnna Lenae Broward, age thirty, born and raised in the Altgeld Gardens Housing Complex on Chicago's far south side, graduated from Howard University with a master's in computer tech. Went on to found the first ever home security network using artificial intelligence. There was an IRS inquiry into the source of her company's initial funding, but nothing ever came of it. She disclosed her financial statements during the ensuing audit, was fined $22 million, and the case was closed."

McKenzie drank from his lukewarm cup of Starbucks coffee and stuck out his lower lip in thought. Meanwhile, Sinclair typed like a mad woman.

"Oh, wow," Sinclair said after a time. "Hm. Interesting."
Her full, pink lips moved to the side. She was an attractive,
young, Black woman, somewhere in her early thirties, with
long, dark eyelashes and a naturally combative disposition.
Erica Sinclair didn't take shit from anyone. Not even the
mayor.

"What is it?" Mackenzie asked.

"Johnna Broward and the alleged suspect, Michael
Caldwell, seem to be from the same Chicago neighborhood.
At least that's what I'm getting from his record. He's been
arrested twice in Altgeld Gardens - once in 2004 for criminal
confinement, kidnapping, illegal possession of a firearm,
and attempted murder. He bonded out and was awaiting trial
on those charges when he and twenty-seven others were
indicted in a RICO conspiracy targeting a set of the Almighty
Black P. Stone Nation that, at the time, was operating out of
Altgeld Gardens. This guy was a violent Chicago gangster.
How he managed to be hired at Panteon is beyond me."

"You think Johnna knew of his criminal history?"

"She *had* to have known. Like I said, they're from the
same housing complex. And I'm pretty sure Panteon isn't
just hiring people off the streets. You've got to be one of the
very best in the tech world to work under Johnna Broward."

"But this guy was a common criminal," McKenzie
muttered matter-of-factly.

"He was. So, the question is, why was he allowed to work
there, and what was it that drove him to murder four of his
coworkers?"

McKenzie nodded his head and drove on. Sinclair was
right. This investigation was already becoming more
interesting than many of their previous cases, and they
hadn't even made it to the crime scene.

Chapter 2
Chicago, Illinois

"Girl, it's hot as hell out here," Nya said, mopping her forehead with the back of her hand. She yanked at the snug crotch of her tight, little, denim shorts and then bit into the crushed ice of her cherry flavored SnoCone.

Her friend, Lacey, bit into a grape-flavored one, and the two of them continued up Chicago Avenue on foot, talking and talking and talking. About their so-called friends. About the boys who were all in their DMs. About the local gangs who were hard at work, trying to murder their rivals for clout. About the cockroach that had gained notoriety at last month's Met Gala before being stomped out on the red carpet.

"Bitch, they had that roach on the Gram with Louis Vuitton skin and everything," Lacey said with raucous laughter. "I died right then and there."

The two twenty-year-old Chicagoans were all smiles. Nya only had $32.55 in her pocket and $40.21 in her Cash App account, but it was more than enough to get through the day. They'd worry about tomorrow when it came. Nya and Lacey were two of the most popular girls in the Austin neighborhood, and there was always a thirsty, young hustler willing to splurge a little to get in good with them.

Lacey was an Amazon - 6'2" and well over two hundred thirty pounds. Most of it was in her ass and thighs. Her lace-front wig was neatly styled into a shoulder-length bob. Her skin was brown and rich like peanut butter with nary a blemish. She wore no underwear beneath her orange and white sundress, allowing her bountiful, round ass to bounce and jiggle freely as they walked down the sidewalk.

Nya, on the other hand, was a tiny little thing, just four feet ten inches in height and barely an ounce over a hundred pounds. She was a bad, young redbone with flawless features and a sexy, petite body that kept her social media comments ablaze with fire and heart-eyed emojis. There were hundreds of men (and more than a few women) in hot pursuit of her. But like Lacey, Nya was single. Fuck nigga free. She could bust out a twerk right in the middle of traffic and not have to worry about it coming back to bite her later on. Her last boyfriend had cheated on her repeatedly, half the time with girls who weren't even slightly attractive, so she'd canceled him and dived headfirst into the single life.

"This boy they call Crunchy just texted me, talkin' 'bout he finna pull up," Lacey said, looking down at her smartphone and working it with one thumb.

"Tell him to come on." Nya wiped her forehead and sighed. "I was about to get us an Uber anyway."

"I'm textin' him back now."

They stopped near the corner of Chicago Avenue and Trumball, and Nya stood, sucking on her sweetly flavored ball of ice and staring into traffic while Lacey worked her thumb. There were a lot of eyeballs on them. DCG Shun of the DCG Brothers rap duo rode past in his blacked-out S-Class Mercedes. He had a girl in the car with him, so Nya only smiled and waved. He smiled back and turned quickly away. Nya rolled her eyes and shifted her gaze to a passing Buick sedan. The driver was Fat Perry, a certified bum who swore up and down he was the plug. He had huge ears with bulbous keloids dangling behind the lobes. He slowed his car to a stop and lowered his window.

"Lacey," he shouted, "when you gon' slide through and bounce all dat ass on a real nigga?"

Nya sucked her teeth and sneered at him in disgust. Lacey glanced up from her phone and without missing a beat said, "When I meet one."

Fat Perry chuckled aloud, as if he hadn't just suffered the hardest curve of the year. "Y'all come on and get out that heat. I'll give y'all a ride back down to Central. No charge."

"We good, boo boo," Nya said with another roll of the eyes.

She was just settling her indignant gaze back on Fat Perry when a sudden screech of tires caused her head to swivel. Lacey looked up at the same time. Three car lengths behind Fat Perry's gray Buick, a blacked-out Dodge Durango had just whipped in front of a dark red Escalade and hit the brakes while a white Chevy Tahoe blocked in the Escalade from the rear. The Escalade was suspended over large chrome rims with razor-thin tires, and its windows were darkly tinted.

The passenger's side doors on the Durango swung open, and two boys jumped out with black Covid masks covering the lower halves of their faces. One of them held an AR-style rifle with a double-drum magazine. The second boy toted a black handgun with a long clip. They ran around to the front of their Durango with their guns aimed at the Escalade's windshield.

"Ohhh, shit," Lacey murmured, taking a step back.

Nya unconsciously took a step backward as well, and she turned a little, ready to take off running in the opposite direction if she heard any gunshots.

But no shots were fired. The driver of the Escalade — a tall, muscular, handsome-looking man with dark skin and deep, shimmering waves in his hair — pushed open his door and stepped out with his hands raised above his head, and the two gunmen climbed in, keeping their guns trained on their carjacking victim until they sped off from the scene.

Several vehicles slowed to a crawl after witnessing the brazen carjacking. One older woman stuck her head out the driver's window of her minivan and asked the unfortunate stranger if he was okay. He ignored her completely. Fat Perry pulled to the side of the road for a brief moment then changed his mind and drove quickly away. Glowering at the three fleeing SUVs, the man dove out of the street and onto the sidewalk.

"That was Cold Gang," Lacey muttered, speaking what Nya was thinking.

Mikey and Derrick Simms were cousins. They were also members of the Cold Gang CVLs, a set of conservative Vice Lords that operated several blocks down. The Durango belonged to Mikey. He had picked up Nya and Lacey and taken them to a Moneybagg Yo concert in it just three days ago, shortly after Nya's ten-year-old Ford Explorer broke down on her on the Eisenhower Expressway. Derrick didn't own a vehicle, so he was always riding with Mikey. Cold Gang was known around the west side of Chicago for carjacking people and using the vehicles to stalk and ultimately gun down their rivals, and Nya was willing to bet her last $72.76 that they had taken the Tahoe just like they'd just taken the Escalade.

"Bitch ass niggas!" the carjacking victim shouted at no one in particular.

He started off toward Nya and Lacey. Nya's mouth hung open in shock as she watched him approach. The man's black T-shirt had Dior printed all over it in red lettering. His fitted jeans and sneakers were clearly high-end designer, and he walked with a gait that Nya found to be both enticing and intimidating. Huge, rolling slabs of muscle filled his arms from wrist to shoulder. His hairline was neat and crisp, as if he'd left his barber's chair no more than an hour ago. He was ten feet away when he noticed the phone in Lacey's hand.

"Ay, shorty," he said, extending his hand, palm up. "Let me use that." And before she had time to respond, he added, "I'll pay you for it. I got a hun'ed for you to let me make a phone call real quick."

He muscled a knot of cash out of his front, left-hand pocket and thumbed a fresh hundred-dollar bill off the top, and Nya noted that there were at least more hundreds under that. She estimated that, if the entire knot of cash consisted of hundred-dollar bills, the man was holding at least five or six grand. She took her smartphone from her back pocket and offered it to the man before Lacey could offer hers.

"Here, you can just use mine," she said.

"How you just gon' step on my toes like that?" Lacey asked.

"Shut up, hoe. You know we ain't gon' do nothin' but spend it together anyway."

It was Lacey's turn to roll her eyes, but the indignant gesture hardly registered in Nya's brain. The man handed her the hundred-dollar bill, and she quickly pocketed it as he thumbed the side button to turn on her phone screen.

"The password's Nya with three a's at the end." She spelled it out for him, eyeing his clean and neatly trimmed fingernails as he swiped the screen and typed in the password. She could smell his cologne from a foot away. The delectable scent of it made her want to take a step closer, but she kept her distance.

"Wonder why they didn't check your pockets," Lacey said to the tall, handsome man as she lowered her eyes back to her phone. "I could see they was fat from the second you started walkin' this way."

The man glared daggers at her. He was obviously seething with rage. If looks could kill, Lacey would have been cremated right there on the spot.

He made a phone call and didn't get an answer, so he typed out a text message and sent that instead. He handed Nya her phone back. As she stood, staring into the passing sea of traffic, his jaw muscles tightened and relaxed. He balled and unballed his fists and flared his nostrils.

"That bitch just set me up," he said finally.

"Who?" Nya asked. "I know everybody out here. Who set you up?"

"Don't get involved in that shit, Nya," Lacey warned. "That ain't none of our business."

Nya's gaze remained on the stranger. She nibbled at one corner of her bottom lip and sighed. "Who set you up?" she repeated, tossing the remainder of her SnoCone into the vacant lot behind her.

The man hesitated, clenching and unclenching his teeth. Nya found it incredibly difficult not to focus on his enormous biceps. The rage coursing through him was palpable. She could almost feel it, constricting her lungs, making it harder to breathe. His Dior shirt seemed to be painted on his chest. Nya spotted a few strands of gray in his goatee. She guessed his age to be somewhere around thirty, maybe thirty-five.

After a long, tense moment, he spoke through clenched teeth. "It was a bitch named Bianca."

Lacey's eyes went wide. Nya gasped and brought a hand up to cover her gaping mouth, and her eyes widened too. She looked at Lacey, Lacey looked at her, and they both turned to gawk at the man standing before them.

He took note of their reactions. Eyes asquint, he lowered his head a few degrees and looked from Nya to Lacey and back to Nya again. He was only an inch taller than Lacey, but he towered over Nya.

"What?" Nya muttered innocently.

He didn't say a word. Two seconds later, someone pulled a royal blue Nissan Altima to the curb and honked the horn, shifting everyone's attention. The dread-headed, young man in the driver's seat looked almost too young to be behind the wheel. He was brown-skinned and relatively handsome. Leaning forward with a Glock pistol on his lap, his dreads were tied in a knot behind his head.

"Welp," Lacey said with a relieved smile. "That's our ride."

She hurried over to the Nissan and pulled open the front passenger door to get in. Nya started to turn toward the car, but the man grabbed hold of her elbow.

"I got five racks if you can tell me who that was who took my truck," he said.

"Wayment, you got *how* much? Five thousand dollars?"

"That's what I said. Five bands. Allah my witness."

Nya didn't hesitate. "Come on," she said and pulled open the rear passenger's side door. "Crunchy, this my boyfriend, Renzo. He's coming to the house with us."

Crunchy nodded. "Hurry up and get it. You know it's up out here. Lord n'em just whacked one of the Royals, and you know Baby T Blood Gang back into it with the Rich Way Cs. It's crackin' 'round this bitch."

There was a car seat in the back, so Nya let the man she'd named Renzo sit down first, and she sat on his lap. Lacey craned her neck to look behind her and rolled her eyes at Nya's gloating smile as the Nissan rocketed forward into traffic.

15

Chapter 3

Renzo's actual name was Lejon Kamari White. Most people who knew him personally called him Grizzy. He'd gone into federal prison a Gangster Disciple and exited four years later a devout Muslim.

Well, a *somewhat* devout Muslim.

He still refrained from eating pork, and he still possessed a certain level of the strict discipline the Islamic teaching had instilled in him over the years, but he no longer prayed five times a day, and he'd gone back to dealing drugs. He'd befriended far too many drug connects in prison not to utilize them for his own personal gain. And besides, there was no way in hell he was going to be working at some low-wage, fast food restaurant. His father was Willie White, the legendary drug kingpin and high-ranking Black P Stone who'd gone Fed in the early 2000s when he was busted with ninety-one kilos of black tar heroin. Grizzy had a family legacy to uphold, and he was well on his way to becoming a street legend in his own right. He'd only been free from prison a total of seventeen months, and he'd already accumulated over four hundred thousand dollars, more than enough drug money to open his own fast-food joint and still have a mountain of cash left over.

Grizzy's whole reason for even visiting the west side of Chicago had everything to do with his incarcerated father. Willie White had asked Grizzy to track down a former member of the Black P. Stones named Devonte "Butch"

Gibbs, a man who had years earlier packed up his family and moved from the Altgeld Gardens apartment complex on the far south side of Chicago to a three-flat on Thomas Street and Keystone Avenue on the city's west side. Grizzy had been stalking out the address for two days now, which was how he'd met Bianca, a cute, young, dark-skinned girl with long, silky hair and a bit of a gut that had protruded over the waistline of her skintight jeans. She'd walked up to the driver's door of his Escalade and asked him for a light, so she could smoke the blunt she had tucked behind her ear, and figuring he might learn something about Butch from a local hood chick like Bianca, he'd offered to smoke a blunt of his own exotic weed with her if she would get in his SUV and smoke her blunt with him.

The idea had proven beneficial to his cause. Bianca was talkative from the start. All he'd done was mention that one of his father's old friends named Butch was married to a woman named Monique Taylor, and three of their young adult children lived in the building with them. The dirty brown, Ford F250 parked in front of the building belonged to Butch. He worked in construction, Monique was a schoolteacher at Whitney Young, and all three of their kids were holding down jobs while completing their college degrees online. They were a nice family, Bianca said, the kind that stayed to themselves and didn't meddle in other people's business.

Soon after the blunts with Bianca, Grizzy had received a call from a south side drug dealer who'd been buying dope from him for months now. He'd had a kilo of fentanyl in a KFC bag on the floor behind his seat, and Bianca had traveled with him back to his old south side neighborhood, where he'd sold the brick for the hefty price of $45,000. He'd let Bianca count out the impressive piles of cash for him, which had clearly excited her.

"The fuck was I thinking?" he muttered vacantly and shook his head.

The girl sitting on his lap turned sideways to look at him. There was plenty of room for her next to the car seat, but he wasn't about to ask her to move. He could tell from her smile that she was feeling him, and it felt good having a bad bitch like her sitting on his lap. But the fact remained that another west side chick had just set him up to be carjacked at gunpoint, and he couldn't stop thinking about it.

Bianca was as slick as oil. Not only had she talked him into moving his pistol from his lap and stashing it in his glove compartment, but she'd also assured him that he had nothing to worry about here on the west side. All the while, she'd been texting on her phone with her "girlfriend." Grizzy was now convinced that the "girlfriend" was one of the gunmen who'd just taken off in his brand-new, 2023 Escalade.

"It's not your fault," the girl on his lap said. She took his chin in her small, delicate hand and ran her thumb back-and-forth along his jawline. "I'll tell you everything when we get to my place, okay? It's right up the street."

Grizzy offered a small nod and rested a hand on her thigh. She smelled like Dove soap and high-grade marijuana. Her lips were tinted red from the SnoCone she'd been sucking on moments earlier. Her tantalizing scent filled his lungs with every breath he took, and he intentionally breathed in deeply to inhale as much of it as humanly possible. She wore a thin, gold necklace around her neck. The attached gold pendant spelled out "Nya" in three-inch-high gold lettering. Her lips were full and moist, her open-mouthed smile revealing two rows of perfect, square teeth. Her long, black hair had a silky texture and gleamed in the sunlight. Grizzy couldn't remember ever seeing a woman who looked as stunningly gorgeous as Nya. No other woman even came close. In order to focus on the situation at hand, he had to literally force himself to look away from her.

Up front, the dread headed young driver Nya had called Crunchy was telling her friend about another shooting that had taken place sometime last night. Someone named Tay Money had shot into a crowd of people in Cold Gang territory. Grizzy had never heard of Cold Gang, but then again, he was from the south side, born in Altgeld Gardens but raised on 72nd and Green. His neighborhood was run by the Dog Pound faction of Gangster Disciples. He'd grown up around drill rapper Lil Durk's older brother, D-Thang, and several other big name street niggas. Grizzy had been a cold young gangster in his teenage years, and although he was a lot more chill now than he was back then, that gangster shit was still in him.

Grinding his teeth in a vicious scowl, he pondered over the things he'd left inside his luxury SUV - his .45 caliber Smith & Wesson pistol, the backpack he'd dropped the $45,000 in, and his iPhone. He was more upset about his phone than anything else. The money could be replaced. So could the gun. But he had so much personal information in the phone. Too many contacts. He could only remember a few phone numbers by heart. He'd tried calling his mother, Alvergia White, but he knew she was likely working at Mount Sinai Medical at this time of day, drawing blood and testing it for various reasons. When she didn't answer, he'd texted his nineteen-year-old daughter, Kamari, telling her that he had been carjacked on Chicago Avenue, that he was safe, and that he would report the truck stolen as soon as he got the chance. He knew Kamari was probably still in bed. She'd stayed up late last night, partying with a few of her best friends at the Costilla Resort and Hotel in Cancun, Mexico. Grizzy figured she wouldn't be up for at least another hour or so.

The more he thought about the carjacking and the bitch he believed was responsible for it, the angrier he became. He'd planned on keeping his mouth shut for the remainder of the ride, but after just wo minutes of silence, the frustration became too overwhelming, and he parted his lips to ask what all she knew about Bianca.

But no words came out because at that very moment, he spotted his Escalade.

It was half a block ahead of them, and it seemed to be in wild pursuit of a money green 80's model Chevy Caprice on oversized gold rims.

Nya gasped and pointed. "Ain't that your..."

The barrel of the AR-style assault rifle appeared from the passenger's window of the Escalade as it pulled alongside the Caprice. Leaning forward, Grizzy was able to actually see the fire explode from the barrel as the unknown shooter sent a hail of bullets into the Chevy's driver side. The Caprice veered sharply to the right, side-swiping a beige-colored minivan, before swerving left into oncoming traffic and colliding head on with an ice cream truck.

The Escalade turned and raced off down Lavergne Avenue. Traffic slowed to a crawl. Grizzy felt his heart pounding against his ribcage. Part of him wanted to jump out and take off running after his fleeing SUV and had he possessed a gun, he very well might have done it.

Crunchy had Twista's classic, *Adrenaline Rush*, playing at low volume. He paused the song, looked over at Nya's friend, and said, "Damn, that was Tay Money in that Chevy."

Chapter 4

It was almost noon when Johnna Broward was transported by ambulance to New York Presbyterian Lower Manhattan Hospital. Kiara Barrington, CFO of Panteon Tech, rode in the back with her, talking and texting on two different iPhones the entire time, and by the time they arrived at the hospital, there were three blacked-out Chevy Surburbans packed near the emergency room entrance. The men who emerged from the SUVs wore expensive, black suits and dark shades. They were large men with serious demeanors and tiny mics in their ears. They could have been Secret Service agents. They scanned the area before EMS personnel rolled Johnna through the sliding doors, and five of them accompanied her and Kiara into the hospital.

The surgical procedure was done in no time. Three stitches in the side of her lower lip and a cranial scan to make sure the impact with her office wall hadn't caused any swelling of the brain. Aside from that, she was fine. She was sitting up in her hospital bed, awaiting her CA scan results, when the two NYPD detectives entered her room.

The man reminded her of CNN's Anderson Cooper, a slender, white man with silver hair and a light smile. He wore a button up shirt and tie with the sleeves rolled halfway up his forearms. His slacks were spiffy, his dress shoes new looking. His hands were in his pockets as he walked in, the gossamer strands of his hair on his forearms glistening in the light. His gaze landed on Johnna and didn't waver.

The woman was another story. If this was a good cop/bad cop scenario, she was undoubtedly the bad one. Her whole face seemed to be one big scowl. She wore a fuchsia blouse over a long, form-fitting skirt and heels. Her eyelashes were three times as long as Johnna's. She looked angry for no reason, the epitome of a mad, Black woman.

Johnna felt a hint of a grin playing at the corners of her mouth. She struggled to suppress it. Standing next to the bed, Kiara crossed her arms over her huge breasts, pursed her lips, and moved her neck from side to side, like a cobra being lured out of a vase. She may have been worth seven figures now, but she was still a hood girl at heart, a product of Chattanooga, Tennessee's College Hill Courts apartments. Light-skinned and heavyset, wrapped in a chic blue one-shouldered Chanel dress with cute white splotches all over it, Kiara Barrington was a chunky, little teddy bear to everyone she loved and an ill-tempered rhino to those who crossed her.

"Uhhh, do we have a problem?" she asked. All attitude.

"I'd say so," said the male detective. "You've got five dead coworkers in your workplace. Three others wounded. Detective Sinclair and I just left the scene. It's a real-life massacre in there."

Johnna experienced a heart wrenching flashback of her flamboyant, gay personal assistant, "Black Ant" Ferguson, fighting with the shooter. She'd been watching the hallway cameras from her office computer when he was shot down. He'd lunged at Caldwell and attempted to get a grip on the assault rifle, and for a fleeting couple of seconds, it seemed like he might succeed. But Caldwell was a huge man, and Black Ant was practically a stick figure. Caldwell had ripped the gun from Black Ant's grasp, shoved him away, and shot him once through the chest and twice through the head.

The traumatizing memory brought a fresh wave of tears to Johnna's eyes. She reached to the left of her bed and picked a tissue from the Kleenex box. She dabbed at her eyes and sniffled.

"I've got nothing to hide," she said shakily. "We fired Caldwell three days ago. Caught him on camera snooping around inside my office two nights in a row. He went peacefully enough. I instructed our president to offer him a generous severance package and to send him on his way. He packed his things and left without a word to anyone. None of us could have predicted him returning to the office in such a rage."

Detective Sinclair, the female cop, produced a small yellow notepad and an ink pen from her breast pocket. She began writing. Kiara sat down in the gray, leather, easy chair next to Johnna's bed and eyed the two detectives like a vigilant watchdog.

The silver-haired detective adjusted the holstered firearm on his hip. He was incredibly gaunt and narrow-waisted, so thin that the pin in his belt was secured in its last hole. The NYPD badge on his belt read Detective R. McKenzie. His badge number was 34417.

"Walk us through what happened," he said. "From the beginning."

"Can't you just watch the surveillance footage?" Johnna asked.

McKenzie nodded. "Your head of security turned that over to us when we arrived on scene. Sinclair and I will have our digital analysts pouring over every second of that footage for the next few weeks. It'll also be sent to Quantico for the FBI to analyze it as well. What we're interested in right now is your version of events. What led to the shooting? What was Caldwell looking for in your office? Why would he gun down all those innocent people, just to make it to your office and stop shooting?"

A cold chill shot through Johnna's diminutive, little body. She stilled herself, got her emotions in check, and stared straight ahead at Detective R. McKenzie.

"I have no idea what led up to this shooting," she said tightly. "Nor do I know why Caldwell found the need to go snooping around in my office. The man was obviously a fucking nutcase."

"Did he say anything to you when he assaulted you in your office?"

Johnna Broward looked at Detective McKenzie and said nothing for eight impossibly long seconds. So long that Detective Sinclair planted her fists on her hips and squinted at Johnna. So long that the CNN anchor on the TV screen across from her bed was able to vice an entire news update on the shooting:

"As you can see from our live aerial feed, the FBI has just descended on the scene at Panteon Tech headquarters where, just moments ago, a deadly workplace shooting claimed the lives of four Panteon employees. The suspect was shot and killed by an armed security guard but not before killing four and wounding three others in New York's deadliest workplace shooting in years. We've just received word that Panteon CEO Johnna Broward was reportedly injured in this incident and transported to a local area hospital. We'll bring you more on this story after the short break."

"No," Johnna said after the unreasonably long pause. "He didn't say anything. He picked me up by my neck and slapped me across the room. If you have any other questions, you can direct them to my personal attorney. Her name's Nikkia Staples of the Bostic and Staples law firm in Chicago. I'm sure you've heard of her."

Detective McKenzie's subtle smirk spread out into an even broader one. Of course he'd heard of Nikkia Staples. She was an attorney to the stars with her most famous client being none other than Alexus Costilla, the Black and Mexican female mogul who had just recently surpassed Elon Musk to become the wealthiest person in the world.

McKenzie nodded once, then he and Detective Sinclair turned to leave. "We'll be seeing you around," he said without looking back.

Johnna shook her head at the departing NYPD detectives. There was no way those two cops would be seeing her around, at least not anytime soon. An hour from now, she planned to be forty thousand feet in the air, soaring west in her Gulfstream private jet, on her way back to Chicago to settle this mess once and for all.

Chapter 5

Lacey gave Crunchy the directions to her and Nya's place on Central Avenue. He parked in the alleyway behind the house, and the four of them filed into the backyard, up a rickety set of wooden porch steps, and into a small, neatly appointed kitchen.

Grizzy plopped down in a chair at the square, wooden table. He dug in his pocket and brought out a tied-off baggie of OG Kush and a pack of Backwoods blunt wraps. Images of the bullet-riddled Chevy Caprice flashed across his mind as he began breaking apart sticky marijuana bud on the bare tabletop. They had driven past the Caprice slowly enough for them to see the flesh and blood splattered all over the dashboard and windshield. A pregnant woman with multiple bullet wounds had pushed open the passenger door and crawled out to the street. Nya had gasped and looked away. Lacey had teared up and muttered a curse. Crunchy and Grizzy hadn't said a word.

Lacey rushed off to the bathroom while Nya opened the fridge and looked inside. She turned to Grizzy. "Renzo, you drink beer, don't you?"

Crunchy sat down across from Grizzy. His unibrow furrowed as he looked from Grizzy to Nya and back to Grizzy. "How she don't know what you drink, and she supposed to be yo' bitch?"

Nya answered the question. "He ain't really my man. I only said that so you could give him a ride. We just met him.

Cold Gang had just jacked him for his 'Lac truck, the same one they just used to shoot up Tay Money's Chevy."

"Yeah, gimme a beer," Grizzy said, ignoring the stunned expression on Crunchy's face.

"Damn, that was yo' shit?" Crunchy asked.

Grizzy only nodded his head. He was far too upset about losing his Escalade to speak on it. Nya placed two cold bottles of Miller Genuine Draft on the table in front of them then cracked open a cold Evian water for herself. She took two long gulps and then rubbed the plastic bottle across her forehead.

"Don't take it personal," Crunchy said, twisting the cap off his beer. "That's how Cold Gang get down. They carjack niggas all the time and use the whips to slide on their opps."

"Naaa," Nya said. "It's deeper than that. Bianca set him up. You know she's Mikey's baby mama, and they jumped out of Mikey's truck. Renzo was just with Bianca. She set him up just like she set up K.J. a few weeks ago."

Grizzy gritted his teeth. His nostrils pulsated with a fiery rage he hadn't felt in years. Just knowing that Bianca had done this before, just weeks prior, infuriated him to no end. Nya's friend, Lacey, returned to the kitchen seconds later with tears in her eyes and her smartphone in hand, talking about how sad it was that Tay Money was dead. She'd gone to high school with him. She'd dated his uncle, Von, for a short while last year. She'd purchased some Roxicodone pills from him just yesterday.

"Renzo, you need to hurry up and report that truck stolen, so they won't be questioning you about Tay Money gettin' killed," Nya said, wrapping a consoling arm around her grieving friend and handing her own smartphone to Grizzy.

So, he did just that. He dialed 9-1-1 and, keeping the details to a bare minimum, filed a police report about his carjacked Escalade. When the woman asked if he knew who the carjackers were, he said no. When she asked if he could describe the suspects' physical features, he said he could not.

And when he ended the call, he looked at the bushy-browed young guy seated across the table from him and said, "I ain't say too much, did I?"

Crunchy shook his head no. "Nah, that was solid. Shit, Nya just told you it was Mikey who robbed you, and you ain't tell that to them people. You good in my book."

With a subtle nod, Grizzy put fire to the end of the thickest blunt he'd rolled all year. He let Nya and Crunchy roll two more blunts, and while they smoked and talked about Tay Money's murder, he smoked and did a few other things on Nya's phone. He logged into his Apple account and shut off his iPhone to keep the jackers from being able to receive his incoming calls and texts. Then, he checked the iPhone tracker and found that his phone was currently on Thomas Street and Keystone Avenue, right where he had met Bianca.

He looked up from the phone screen and sat there thinking. Then, he logged out of his Apple account, handed the phone back to Nya, and said, "Bianca lives on Thomas and Keystone, right?"

Nya nodded. "Mmm hm. With her mama, her brother, Marvell, and her two trifling ass sisters. Oh, and all their kids. They got like eight or nine of them lil nappy headed fuckers." She looked at Crunchy. "He got five bands for the lo' on Derrick and Mikey."

"I definitely got that," Grizzy said. He turned up his beer and downed half of it in three big gulps. He wiped his mouth and burped and said excuse me. Nya flashed a smile at him, and he added, "Matter of fact, I got five thousand for that address, and I got five more for a gun and a ride over there. Them lil niggas got me fucked up. I was a big stepper before they even learned how to walk."

Crunchy's one long eyebrow rose up into his forehead, like a furry, black caterpillar moving sideways. He regarded Grizzy with a disbelieving stare. Then, he took a Glock pistol with an extended magazine from his waist and his car keys from his pocket. He placed them on the table and slid them toward Grizzy. "She know where Mikey and Derrick live," he said.

Nya reached for the keys. "I'll drive," she said. "I ain't never liked them Cold Gang niggas anyway. They shot my cousin, Lenny, at a Halloween party last year. And that bitch, Bianca, got me and Lacey jumped by some of her friends on prom night. I can't stand that hoe."

Grizzy took the knot of hundred-dollar bills out of his pocket and began counting out the money on the table. He'd left the house with $12,000 in bank - new hundreds in one front pocket and $5,000 in fifties in his other front pocket. He'd broken a hundred at IHOP for breakfast, and tipped the waitress all of the change, and he'd given another hundred to Nya to use her phone, so he knew there was exactly $11,800 in his stack of hundreds. He counted out fifty of them, and slid the pile toward Crunchy, then counted out another fifty and passed them to Nya. She left the kitchen with her cash in hand and returned moments later with a light blue, leather purse on her shoulder.

Lacey began ogling the pile of hundreds Crunchy was thumbing his way through, and suddenly, she didn't look so grief stricken. She sniffled and wiped her eyes, grabbed a can of Pepsi out of the fridge, and had Crunchy follow her back to her bedroom.

Five minutes later, Nya and Grizzy were back in the Altima, only this time they were in the front seats. Grizzy sat in the passenger seat with the Glock under his thigh. Nya started the engine, buzzed her seat forward, and adjusted the rearview mirror.

"Please don't get me shot or arrested," she said, looking over at Grizzy as he reclined in his seat. "I ain't tryna die young, and I damn sure ain't tryna go to jail."

"You'll be safe with me, shorty. On Larry Bernard Hoover, I ain't gon' let nothin' happen to you." Grizzy licked his lips and forced a smile. "Just drive."

Chapter 6

"Mikey and Derrick live right up the street from Bianca," Nya said. "In a white house on Keystone. It used to be Double-I territory, but the Cold Gang CVLs took over that whole lil section a few years ago. My daddy told me about it. He used to be heavy in the streets around here."

Grizzy nodded his head. He peeled off his shirt and tied it strategically around his head, creating a makeshift mask that covered everything but his bloodshot eyes. He was tall, dark, and chiseled like a steroid abuser, and Nya couldn't stop glancing over at his rock-hard chest and abdomen as he fixed the shirt on his head. The rippling bricks of muscle in his six-pack made her mouth water. The veins in his arms were like cords, fat and serpentine, snaking a path down from his shoulders to his wrists. His biceps were enormous, like a pro wrestler's.

Nya reached over and gave his left forearm a squeeze; she couldn't help herself. Her hand traveled up to his mighty shoulder and then wandered down his herculean chest, pausing to fully enjoy the intimidating feel of sharply defined abdominal muscles.

"How often do you work out?" she asked.

"Six days a week." He ejected the extended magazine in his newly acquired Glock pistol and eyed the fat .45 caliber bullets before reinserting the clip into the bundle. The gun was equipped with red laser sighting. He flicked on the laser beam and aimed at the dashboard in front of him. "I take Fridays off and get it in on all the other days."

"It shows." Reluctantly, Nya returned her hand to the steering wheel. "So, what were you doing over there with Bianca in the first place? And put that gun down until it's time to use it. If I ride past one of the CPD's Tahoes, they'll be able to look right down into this car and see that gun. Then what?"

He chuckled twice, but he listened, slipping the gun back under his leg.

"My pops asked me to go over there and find somebody," he said. "Papa was a drug kingpin and a general for the Stones. One of his boys was holdin' a lot of his money when they got indicted. That's whose house I was watchin' when I met Bianca."

"How much money was he holdin'?"

He shrugged his massive shoulders. "Pops only said it was a lot. I think he wanted to tell me how much it was, but he don't trust that phone line. He just bought a cell phone in the Fed joint they got him in, and he feel like the officer who sold it to him might be on some setup type shit. Like maybe they tapped the phone and put it in his hands to see what all they could get."

"He was smart to do that." Nya swerved around an idling tow truck. Its driver was in the process of repossessing a booted Buick Park Avenue. She was on Division Street because taking Chicago Avenue would have undoubtedly meant crossing the paths of numerous police vehicles.

Yet and still, she observed several CPD squad cars slicing this way and that way, whipping around other motorists with little to no regard for existing traffic laws. She found herself checking and rechecking the speedometer, driving as she had during that first nerve-wracking driver's test she'd taken four years ago.

"We're almost there," she said, chancing another quick glance at her passenger's mouthwatering physique. "What do people call you? I heard you say Lejon White when you made that police report, but do you got a nickname?"

He looked over at her and stared. She couldn't know for sure, but she thought she sensed a smile behind the portion of his Dior shirt that covered the lower half of his face.

"Wouldn't be wise to give you my name when I know I'm about to whack somebody right in front of you," he said after a time.

"If I wanted to snitch on you, I could just give the police your real name. Dumbass." She said it with a little smile.

He chuckled merrily. "It's Grizzy," he said. "When I was a lil kid, all I wanted to do was get money, just like my old man. So, I would hustle in school all the time, sellin' popcorn and honey buns and candy, anything I could buy from the store and sell for double in the school cafeteria. In middle school, I moved to weed and cigarettes, and in high school, I sold weed, pills, cocaine, fake IDs — you name it, I sold it. Everybody said I stayed on my grizzy — on my grind, you know — and that's how I got the name."

"I like Lejon better," Nya said decidedly. She drove on in silence for a few blocks, trying vehemently to think about anything but the imminent crime scene she was driving toward. The closer they got to Keystone Avenue, the more jittery she became.

She focused her thoughts on the five thousand dollars she had in her purse. That gave her a small boost of confidence. Her trusty old Ford Explorer had been impounded when she couldn't afford to get it towed off the Eisenhower, but now, she had enough cash to pay those tow fees, the outstanding parking tickets, the automated red-light violation tickets, *and* the ridiculously expensive storage fees. She had initially given up on the possibility of ever having that truck in her possession again. Her ex-boyfriend, Deshawn, had sent her the money to pay the fees two weeks ago, but she'd been a month behind on her rent, and a roof over her head was much more important than transportation.

"Just drive past Mikey and Derrick's spot," Grizzy said, jarring Nya from her reverie. "So, I can see the house. I tracked my phone to Keystone and Thomas, so I'm pretty sure that's where they went after they shot up that Chevy. Prob'ly went to Bianca's crib."

Nya nodded her head and stilled herself for what was to come. She turned onto Keystone and pointed out the white clapboard house where Mikey and Derrick lived. She knew that the house had once belonged to Nate Hutchins, the former king of the Imperial Insane Vice Lords, also known as the Double Is. There was a short, chubby, brown-skinned man standing on the front porch, holding a lit cigarette between the first and second fingers of his left hand, while he pounded on the screen door with his right foot.

"Who is that?" Grizzy asked, leaning forward a little to study the man on Mikey's front porch.

"They call him Red Rum. He used to be a Double I, but he flipped to a CVL when Nate went down, and Cold Gang took over."

Grizzy didn't have any more questions concerning Red Rum. He laid back in his seat, holding the Glock in his hand again, his gaze fixed on the tinted glass of the sunroom overhead. Nya could feel her heart thumping about three times faster than normal. Her breathing was shaky with adrenaline. She spotted Mikey's black Dodge Durango parked in front of Bianca's house up ahead and briefly considered slamming her foot down on the brake and backing up and jumping out, leaving Grizzy to handle this bullshit on his own.

But she didn't stomp down on the brake. She taped Grizzy's gigantic left arm and said, "Okay, here it is. That's Mikey's truck right there. I think he's in the house with Bianca."

Grizzy sat up and squinted at the Durango as Nya pulled to the curb three houses down from Bianca's place. Nya looked around too, searching the block for other Cold Gang members. There was a drug house just across the street from the gray and white clapboard house where Bianca lived, but Cold Gang only served their customers out the back door, so there was no one out front. A teenage girl in tan cargo shorts and a tube top pushed a stroller on Bianca's side of the street. She had another teenage girl with her. Nya recognized them from the neighborhood, but she didn't know their names.

A short, wrought-iron fence surrounded Bianca's front yard. Bikes and balls and toy guns littered the poorly maintained lawn. A toddler wearing nothing but a heavy looking diaper stood alone amongst the toys, his head swiveling from the dirty orange ball on his left to the plastic Nerf gun on his right, as if struggling to decide which one suited him best.

"That's her house right there," Nya said, pointing. "The gray and white one with the baby in the yard." She paused, nibbled at her thumbnail, then added, "Please don't hit that baby. Whatever you do, just make sure you don't hit him."

"I won't."

Nya waited a couple of seconds and said, "What are you gon' do? Try to get your phone back? Make them tell you where they ditched your truck?"

"Nah. They can keep all that shit. I just want some get back."

Nya thought about that for a short moment. Worried that someone might see her face and recognize her, she reached into the backseat, snatched an infant's blanket out of the car seat, and folded it in half to tie it around the lower half of her face.

She was securing the knot behind her head when the screen door on Bianca's front porch swung open.

Mikey walked out with a red backpack hanging down from his left hand. He was followed out by Derrick and another boy Nya couldn't remember ever seeing before. Then, Bianca and her older sister, Nataya, walked out onto the porch. There wasn't a frown in the bunch. Bianca was counting through a handful of cash as they descended the porch steps. So was Nataya.

Nya turned to Grizzy and asked, "Did they get all that money from you?"

"Drive," Grizzy barked. "Pull up right next to em. I'ma jump out, drill these niggas, and jump back in. All you gotta do is stop, wait, and pull off when I get back in the car. You wit' me?"

Nya sucked in a deep nasal breath and blew it out through parted lips. Then, she stepped down on the gas pedal, and they jetted off from the curb.

Chapter 7

Grizzy had very little faith in Nya's ability to remain cool under pressure. She looked more nervous than a wanted fugitive at an FBI convention. He wished he could have had more time to prep her for the mission, but he'd never been the one to wait things out. The time for retaliation was now, and there was no sense in postponing the inevitable.

He identified the two boys who'd carjacked him by their outfits. They both glanced at the speeding car as it closed in on them, and the boy in the rear reached for his waist as Nya brought the Altima to a lurching stop right next to the Durango. Grizzy had his door open before the car had even stopped. He jumped out and ran around the rear end of the Durango with the Glock raised and aimed at his three male targets just as they reached the sidewalk.

He pulled the trigger and was almost surprised by the fully automatic spray of the .45 caliber rounds. He'd noticed the small square button at the back of the gun when he bought it, and he knew it was a Glock switch, which converted the semi-automatic pistol into a fully automatic machine gun, but this was his first time actually firing a Glock with a switch. The bullets came out much too rapidly to maintain a steady aim, so he merely waved the pistol from side to side as he held the trigger.

The boy, who'd reached for his waist, managed to draw a similar-looking Glock pistol from under his shirt, but before he could raise it, he caught a number of bullets to his upper chest area and fell backward onto the wrought-iron fence.

The two boys who'd carjacked Grizzy were the next to be cut down. He swept his arm to the left, and great mists of red exploded out their backs. The boy holding the backpack — he was brown-skinned and heavyset, like the Red Rum fellow, only instead of a fade he had cornrows — caught at least a few rounds to the face. Grizzy knew this for certain because the boy's head jerked back from the impact, and he fell dead right there on the sidewalk. The other guy stumbled sideways and collapsed against the Durango with numerous bullet holes in his plain white T-shirt.

It took just two seconds for the fully extended magazine to empty. Only then did Grizzy realize that Bianca had also been shot. She lie at the foot of the porch steps with both hands pressed against her stomach. Blood seeped out between her splayed fingers. The cash she'd been counting so proudly just a moment prior surrounded her on the steps. Her older sister had just snatched up the toddler and was fleeing into the house, still holding her share of the loot in one tightly clenched fist.

Grizzy picked up his backpack and the gun that had been dropped by his first victim. He glowered at Bianca, pondering whether he should shoot her again. In the head this time. She most certainly deserved it. But in a split second, he decided against it.

He had just turned and started running back to the car when, out of the corner of his eyes, he saw that the fat guy who'd been pounding at Mikey's front door seconds earlier was now running down the sidewalk in his direction with a gun in one hand. Grizzy got one foot in the passenger door, aimed the Glock he'd lifted off his shooting victim over the roof, and sent a barrage of gunfire up the street.

Phop! Phop! Phop! Phop! Phop! Phop! Phop! Phop!

Red Rum ducked for cover alongside a Hyundai SUV, and Grizzy squeezed off four more shots that tore through the Hyundai's hood and windshield.

"Get in!" Nya yelled.

Grizzy got in, and Nya sped off before he could even get his door shut, both of them lowering their heads as Red Rum returned fire. Then, a brave, young dread head with a Draco ran out from beside a house they were racing past and opened fire. The Altima's back window shattered, and Nya screamed at the top of her lungs as she made a right turn ono a side street and stomped on the gas.

Chapter 8

The Gulfstream 650 had just reached cruising altitude, and Johnna Broward was already on her feet, pacing barefoot along the center aisle as she pushed her Apple AirPods into her ears and phoned her attorney.

Nikkia Staples picked up on the second ring. "Oh, my God, Johnna. Are you okay?"

"I'm fine. I'll need a new tooth, I've got three stitches in my lips, and the side of my head hurts like a bitch, but I'll live."

"Jesus Christ. What the hell happened? I'm looking at MTN News, and they're saying the suspect was a career criminal who was actually employed by Panteon until three days ago. Did you know him? I mean, did you know about his criminal history?"

"Of course I knew about it. I'm the one who hired him."

"Well, excuse my language, but what the *fuck* were you thinking?"

Johnna signed and stopped in her tracks to look up at one of the Gulfstream's four, sixty-inch, high-definition televisions. Every one of them were on MTN News. There was currently an old mugshot of Michael Caldwell on the screen. MTN News anchor Alexandria Ray was informing the public of Caldwell's lengthy rap sheet.

"I'll tell you what I was thinking." Johnna returned to her seat, picked up her half-gallon bottle of Hennessy cognac, and turned it up like a sailor. She drank down a good eight to ten ounces in several throat-bulging gulps then slammed the bottle down on her Egyptian mahogany table and said, "He was from Altgeld Gardens, Nikkia. I thought I was doing a good deed, hiring a Black man from my old neighborhood. He used to run with my older brother. I hired Caldwell fresh out of prison as a favor for a friend. Made him a night shift janitor and started him off at forty-two bucks an hour. He was probably the highest paid janitor in the fucking country."

"So, what went wrong? What made him snap?"

He found out my secret, Johanna thought to herself. It was the one secret she knew she'd never share with anyone else, not even her lawyer. There were only two other people who knew about it. One of them was locked away in a federal prison, and she knew he'd never tell a soul.

The other one was the man who'd pleaded with her to hire Michael Caldwell in the first place, and now, she had a pretty good idea why he'd done it.

"I can't say what it was that made him snap," Johnna said, reclining in her seat and studying her impeccably pedicured toes. She had on a black and gold pair of Versace leggings with a matching sports bra. Her Versace running shoes were under the table. "And to be honest, I really can't say much more over the phone. Where can we meet? I'll be in Chicago by four o'clock Eastern."

"That's three here. I'm at MTN Studios now. They want me to go on with Alexandria Ray at two and speak on your behalf. CNN wants me on at five. Everyone's talking about the suspect's criminal history and wondering how he managed to get hired by one of the world's leading software companies. We have to get out in front of this, Johnna. You're gonna have lawsuits from the families of the victims, lawsuits from surviving employees, inquiries from investors. I know it's still early, and everything's still kind of fresh, but as soon as you get yourself together, I'm gonna need you to get in front of the public and speak from the heart. If you don't do that soon, Panteon stocks can take a huge hit."

"Panteon will be fine. You worry too much. Go on there and do your thing. I'll call you when I land."

Johnna ended the call and went to her Instagram app to view all the concerned direct messages that were pouring in from her close friends and family members. Her page had eighteen million followers, and many of them were posting well wishes in her comments. Deciding it was much too early to be posting about the deadly shooting, she exited the app and went to her list of contacts.

When she found the name of the man who'd talked her into hiring Michael Caldwell over ninety days ago, she drew in a deep breath and dialed the number, hoping the cognac coursing through her veins would be enough to prepare her for the ensuing argument.

And there was surely going to be an argument.

While the phone rang, she looked across the aisle at Jayvon Sullivan, the handsome, young man who'd saved her life today. He was on his phone, video chatting with his wife and their newborn daughter. The wife was in tears. Jayvon kept telling her that everything was fine and that he'd see her as soon as he returned from Chicago later tonight. His boss (Johnna) had just promoted him to her full-time security detail with a starting annual salary of $120,000, and now, they'd have the money to get that condo they'd looked at in Manhattan's coveted Upper East Side.

The wife was a gorgeous, Dominican woman named Estrella. Johnna had seen her on Jayvon's phone screen, and on his Facebook page, and on his Instagram, and Snapchat, and TikTok pages. Johnna had come across the cute, young couple while scrolling through the pics and videos listed under Instagram's #CouplesGoals hashtag, and she'd known right away that Jayvon, a fitness trainer at the time, would be a perfect fit for Panteon. He looked kind of like Lebron

James, a tall, brown man with a full beard and an athletic build.

Johnna had plans to fuck him one day soon. A one-night stand would be fine with her, but she had her mind set on taking him from his wife and keeping him for herself.

"Hi," Johnna said, an ingratiating grin spreading across her attractive brown visage. "Long time no see, Butch."

Chapter 9

They ditched the Altima in an alleyway near Division Street and Central Park Avenue, and Grizzy used his credit card to order an Uber. Their ride arrived less than five minutes later, a curly-haired, older, Black woman in a black Kia Telluride with a soothing Gerald Levert song playing from its sound system.

Clearly shaken by the traumatic Keystone Avenue shooting and their breathtaking escape, Na leaned her head against Grizzy in the backseat and didn't speak, though she did text her friend, Lacey. The driver first took them to a nearby Apple store, where Grizzy used his store credit and insurance to purchase himself a brand-new iPhone. Then, the woman drove them to Grizzy's spacious brownstone home on 81st and Prairie, and he tipped the driver $50.

Walking up the inclined walkway, which ran alongside Grizzy's driveway, Nya looked over at the fleet of vehicles parked there in front of the two-car garage - a dark blue Chevy Corvette, a gray Jeep Grand Cherokee Trailhawk, and a black Dodge Challenger Hellcat Demon.

"These yours?" Nya asked.

Grizzy nodded his head. He had his red backpack on one shoulder, his house keys in one hand, and his new iPhone in the other, texting back-and-forth with his daughter, who had finally awakened to reply to his text message. She'd also messaged her mother, Joya Kelly, who was married to another man and living somewhere in Ohio but still couldn't

43

seem to keep her nose out of Lejon White's business, so now, Joya was texting him too. With a frustrated sigh, he pocketed the phone, unlocked and pushed open his front door, and went to the Panteon security keypad to type in his password.

Nya walked in and gaped at the hardwood flooring and the clear-glass staircase leading up to the second floor. "Oh, you got big money," she said, holding her hips. A hint of a smile lifted the corners of her pretty mouth.

"I got a lil some'n. Not too much."

He led Nya into the living room of his 3,200-square-foot home. The ninety-inch TV screen turned on when they entered the room. The furniture was blue leather, with a darker blue Gucci area rug beneath the glass-top coffee table and blue Gucci blankets draped over the sofas. The base of the table was a red-eyed, black panther with its sharp, white teeth bared menacingly at its invisible prey.

The last channel Grizzy had watched on the massive television was MSNBC, and now, MSNBC's *Symone Show* was on with its best reporting and breaking news of yet another mass shooting, this one perpetrated at Panteon Tech's headquarters in Lower Manhattan. It was reportedly the 227th mass shooting this year.

Nya diverted her gaze to the toes of her cute, little, wedge sandals. Sensing the Keystone Avenue shooting might have something to do with her disinterest in the news, Grizzy picked up the remote from the arm of the sofa and turned to BET+'s *College Hill: Celebrity Edition*. Joseline Hernandez was all in Tiffany "New York" Pollard's face about something.

"You hungry? Thirsty?" Grizzy asked.

Nya crossed her arms and shook her head. When she looked up, she was wearing that hint of a smile again. God, she was beautiful. Grizzy studied her pie-shaped visage for a long moment and realized he really hadn't taken the time to admire her jaw dropping beauty until now. He'd been experiencing pure chaos from the second he first laid eyes on her, and he was only now beginning to see Nya for the incomparably gorgeous little woman she was. She had juicy, red lips and eyes that were slanted like an Asian's. Her ears were small and perfectly formed. Her nose was slender with a tiny, gold ball pierced through the left nostril. She didn't possess much of an ass, but there was a nice curvature to it. Her breasts looked big on her diminutive, little body. Now that her attention-grabbing features were finally registering in Grizzy's brain, he found it difficult not to imagine himself picking her up and feeling her legs wrap snugly around his waist, kissing and sucking on her sexy lips as he carried her into his master bedroom.

"Stop looking at me like that," she said, rolling her pretty eyes.

Grizzy grinned. "I know *exactly* what *you* need."

He left the living room for the kitchen and returned seconds later holding a chilled bottle of lime-flavored Cîroc vodka and two short ball glasses. He sat down at one end of the sofa and filled both glasses almost to the rim, watching Nya from the corner of his eye as she came around the sofa, picked up the TV remote, and made herself comfortable beside him, kicking off her sandals and pulling her legs up beneath her. He offered her a glass and snatched it back when she reached for it.

"You are twenty-one, right?"

Nya's eyelids became narrow slits. "You got the nerve to card me after I just watched you shoot *every*-damn-body?" She reached out and tore the glass from his grasp. "And for your information, I'm only twenty, but I'll be twenty-one in exactly—" She paused to look at the time on her phone— "ten hours and two minutes."

"How old were you when you started drinking?" Grizzy asked. He placed the cold Cîroc bottle on the floor between his designer sneakers, took a drink from his glass, and unzipped his red Nike backpack. "Don't tell me thirteen or no shit like that."

"Fourteen actually." Nya snickered mischievously. "I started kinda late."

Grizzy shook his head, genuinely displeased. He opened the backpack, removed the two Glock pistols, and dumped the remaining contents onto the sofa between Nya and him. There were rubber-banded bundles of fives, tens, twenties, fifties, and hundreds. He eyed the cash bundles and roughly estimated that there was only five to ten grand missing, more than likely just five which was probably what Mikey and Derrick had given to Bianca and Nataya.

"So, they *did* get that money from you," Nya said, sipping. "Shit, man. That's a lot of fuckin' money." She slapped her knee and snickered again. "Listen to me. I sound like ol' girl off *Set It Off*, don't I? *I need that money, Frankie!*"

Grizzy cracked up, laughing. It had been a long time since he'd last seen that great American classic. He removed the extended magazines from the two Glocks and jacked the slides to clear the barrels of ammunition. One was already emptied, and a single bullet jumped from the chamber of the other. He placed the guns on the table and sat back on the sofa, feeling relaxed for the first time in hours. He was home, in a gated community on the south side of Chicago that was much safer than the Windy City's more poverty-stricken neighborhoods. He'd lost a few grand, but he'd stepped on the people responsible for his loss.

Now, he was sitting here with the most beautiful redbone he'd ever seen in his life. She had a glorious little smirk on her face as she sat scrolling through her Instagram messages. She put down her phone, turned to him, and said, "This boy I know from high school just messaged me, askin' if he could eat my ass. Now mind you, this nigga got a whole fiancée and three kids at home, but he wanna stick his tongue up my lil booty."

Grizzy laughed again. "That's that new generation," he said though he knew of several men he'd grown up around who'd been eating ass for decades. "You prob'ly like that nasty shit."

Nya's brow rose, and her smirk became a full-on smile.

"See." Grizzy pointed an accusatory finger. "I knew it. Yo' lil nasty ass."

"Hey, it feels good to me. First time I had a nigga do that shit was Valentine's Day last year. A nigga named Big Worm. He was older than you, I think. He got killed last July on 16th and Trumball. That man took me to a hotel room downtown, one of those nice penthouse suites way up on the top floor. He fixed me a nice, hot, bubble bath, fed me strawberries, and after all that romantic shit, he put his whole tongue in my ass. Mmm. I'm getting' wet just thinkin' about that night."

"Which one feels better, getting' your pussy ate or—"

"Oh, definitely my pussy," she said, cutting him off before he could even finish the question. "That's like the best feeling in the whole wide world. Especially when a man knows what he's doing down there. I like it when a man sucks and licks on my clit while he fingers me at the same time. That shit'll have me gushin' like a fire hydrant."

Grizzy opened his mouth to ask her if she enjoyed giving head and if she thought she was any good at it, but his phone rang before he could voice the question. He looked at his phone screen and, seeing that it was his father calling, quickly rose to his feet.

There was a notable bulge in the front of his jeans. Nya stared at it without commenting though her open-mouthed smile spoke volumes.

"I gotta take this call," he said. "Call your friend and let her know you're good. And don't tell nobody my address."

Nya rolled her eyes and went back to staring at his impressive bulge until he turned to leave the room, and then, she picked up her phone and drank from her glass while he stepped out into the foyer and answered the call.

Chapter 10

When Lacey's phone rang at precisely 2:03 p.m., her legs were still trembling from the orgasm she'd just experienced, and Crunchy was rising from between her meaty brown thighs, his mouth wet and shiny with her juices.

"Oh, shit. Oh, my God. That felt so fuckin' good." She reached up and grabbed him from behind the neck, bringing his mouth down to hers for a brief, passionate kiss. "Mmm. You gon' make a bitch fall in love with that head."

Lacey's bedroom was a lot less organized than Nya's. The ashtray on her nightstand was crammed full of blunt roaches and cigarette butts, and it was surrounded by empty Pepsi cans and tequila bottles. A Hostess cupcake wrapper lay open on the floor next to her overflowing trash can. Her closet was in disarray, and her laundry bin was filled almost to the top with dirty clothes.

Crunchy began slapping his rock-hard erection on her engorged clitoris as she grabbed her phone off the nightstand. It was an Instagram video call from Nya. She sighed and, with a dramatic flutter of the eyelids, answered the call.

"I'm glad you called," she said, halfway out of breath. "I just got off the phone with Latoya from over there on Keystone a few minutes ago. She say her brother, Red Rum, just got shot in a shootout over there, and that Mikey, Derrick, and another Cold Gang nigga named Dre got killed.

Bianca in the hospital. She got hit in the stomach. They say she might have to get one of them shit bags."

Nya only shook her head. She wasn't being her usual talkative self, and Lacey figured it was because the man Nya had nicknamed Renzo was somewhere nearby. Nya had texted her a short while ago, saying she was okay and that she was in an Uber with Renzo. She hadn't even mentioned the shooting.

"Are you okay?"

Nya nodded. "Tha one nigga brought me back to his house after everything went down. I'm good though." She held a glass up for Lacey to see. "Sippin' on this good Cîroc."

"Don't blow none of that money. You know we still gotta go and get Exie out the impound." Lacey had started calling Nya's Explorer "Exie" some time last year, and the name had stuck.

"Bitch, why are you sweatin' like that?" Nya asked.

Lacey switched to the rear camera just as Crunchy was easing his dick in between her saliva-coated vaginal lips. When she switched back to the front-facing camera, Nya's mouth was wide open.

"He gave me a thousand dollars outta that five racks too," Lacey said proudly. She glanced across the room at the pile of hundreds on her dresser. "Girl, let me call you back."

"Okay. Just hit me when y'all done."

Lacey tossed her phone aside and lifted one leg onto Crunchy's scrawny left shoulder. He was just beginning to establish a rhythm, going in deep and coming nearly all the way out before doing it all again, when his phone began to ring. He'd left it face up at the front of the bed. He picked it up and knitted his brow, turning the screen toward Lacey, so she could see what had him looking so puzzled. It was a FaceTime call from Frenchy, a Cold Gang member who was known for catching his rivals lacking and filling them with holes. Crunchy moved back on his knees to answer the call, his dick slipping out of Lacey as he did it.

He accepted the video call, and in the reflection of her dresser mirror, Lacey saw something on his phone that terrified her - a room full of masked men, all of them aiming guns at the camera. At least five of them toted 7.62-milimeter Draco pistols.

"You know what's up, bitch ass nigga. We seen you on the Avenue in that lil Nissan before Lord n'em got hit up on Keystone. We know it was you. It's up there now, nigga. Drop that location. We tryna send you up today."

Crunchy sucked his teeth. "Man, get the fuck off my phone," he said and ended the call before more could be said. He put on a brave face, but Lacey could see right through it. He was clearly worried. His dick was going soft between his skinny legs, and his gaze kept wavering from the phone to the Glock pistol he'd laid at the foot-end of the bed before going down on her. The gun looked just like the one he'd sold to Renzo, from the long-extended clip to the small square button on the back.

He got up and started to dress. "I gotta go," he said drably.

"Don't tell me you're about to walk somewhere."

"My nigga, Vinnie, stay right around the corner on Iowa and Pine. I'll be good. He'll give me a ride back to the block." Crunchy was a member of the Wicket Town faction of Traveling Vice Lords, a gang that dominated the Leamington Avenue area where he lived. He was low on the totem pole within the Wicked Town gang, but he was loved and respected, and Lacey knew his gang would ride for him without question.

Sitting up, Lacey pulled on her Fashion Nova summer dress. She was unable to repress the emotionally paralyzing fear that burgeoned in her chest as she sat, listening to Crunchy make phone call after phone call, informing his gang of the situation. Lacey couldn't wait for him to leave. She wanted him out of her and Nya's place as soon as possible before some Cold Gang member figured out where he was and stopped by for a visit.

She left the bedroom to soap up a washcloth and clean herself in the bathroom sink, a hoe bath. When she came out of the bathroom a few minutes later, Crunchy was fully dressed and standing in the living room, peeking out through the venetian blinds.

"Whose car was that anyway?" Lacey asked, scissoring her legs and leaning against the wall with her arms folded across her chest.

Crunchy shrugged his narrow shoulders. He had released his dreads from the top knot, and they hung down around his head like branches on a willow tree. He was holding his pistol down at his side.

"I got that car off 118th and Perry a few days ago," he said. "Some bitch left it runnin' and went in the house. Me and my nigga hopped in that bitch and drove off."

"What are you waiting for?"

"Vinnie comin' to pick me up. He don't want me walkin' nowhere. And I just texted one of the Ts off Tay Money block and let him know it was Cold Gang who whacked him. That way, we'll be slidin' on Cold Gang together."

"Increase your odds of winning," Lacey said, nodding her head in understanding of his logic.

He turned away from the window seconds later with a glimmer of urgency in his eyes, and Lacey knew right then that his ride had arrived out front.

"I'm gone," he said.

Lacey nodded once, and Crunchy started out the front door, not even bothering to pull it shut behind him nor did he bother concealing his pistol. At this point, he'd probably welcome an arrest.

Crossing the room to the open doorway, Lacey watched him slip into the passenger's side of a silver BMW sedan with tinted windows. When it drove off, she pushed the door shut, locked it, and breathed a huge sigh of relief.

"I told you to mind your fuckin' business, Nya," Lacey muttered heatedly. "Now look at the shit you done started. Got Crunchy runnin' for his life, and on top of that, you done fucked up my whole dick appointment."

She looked down and noticed her erect nipples protruding from the thin fabric of her summer dress. She was still aroused, but she was in no mood to call anyone over. There was too much tension in the streets. She needed some time to herself. And besides, she had a vibrating ten-inch dildo in her top drawer that hadn't been put to use in days.

Walking back to her bedroom, she thought of the thousand dollars resting on her dresser and immediately started spending it in her head. She planned to get herself a gel manicure and a nice pair of shoes for Nya's birthday celebration tomorrow. She would pay her phone bill, buy herself a fifth of tequila, set aside a few hundred to help out with next month's rent, and save the rest for a rainy day. She was due to start working at a local meat packing factory Monday morning, making $18.50 an hour, and she'd need money to get to and from work. Nya would undoubtedly be getting Exie out of the impound, but Nya was looking for another job too, so Lacey knew she wouldn't be able to depend on those free rides for long.

She made it to her bedroom doorway and froze. Her mouth fell open. She grabbed her hips and tilted her head to the side.

The stack of hundred-dollar bills was gone from her dresser.

"That bitch ass nigga," she murmured in disbelief.

Chapter 11

By the time Grizzy returned to the living room, Nya had already refilled her glass once, and she was well on her way to finishing off her second glass.

She'd been scrolling through Facebook ever since she got off the video call with Lacey. Everybody on the west side of Chicago seemed to either be talking about the double murder of Tay Money and his pregnant girlfriend or the triple homicide that had taken place on Keystone Avenue.

Nya was still shaken by the shooting. She'd been around gang violence all her life but never had she been involved in an actual murder. She didn't know what to think. She'd always favored older men, and Lejon was as fine as they came, but could she trust a man who could murder three people in cold blood and go on about his day as if nothing happened?

Grizzy sat down next to Nya and eyed her for a long moment. She had taken the cash he'd dumped on the sofa next to her and separated it into five neat piles on the table, and now, she was watching the episode of *College Hill* on the largest television screen she'd ever seen up close.

"Stop staring at me," she said to Lejon without even looking at him.

In her peripheral, she caught a glimpse of his devilishly handsome grin.

"You got OCD or some'n?" He gestured toward the cash she'd arranged on the table.

"I just hate a mess. Lacey has been my best friend since first grade, but she's a slob, and I'm always fussing with her about it. You dumped the money on the couch and just left it there. I organized it. Simple as that, *Lejon*."

"Damn. That's what we on? Government names?"

"I'm still tryna figure out why you had to go to another room to talk on the phone. You trust me to be your getaway driver, but you don't feel like you can talk in front of me?"

He chuckled and shook his head. He picked up his drink and took a generous swallow. When he spoke again, he sounded a lot more serious than before.

"That was my old man. He got life in the Feds, and he can only pull out his cell phone at certain times of the day. He wanted to know about ol' boy on Keystone. The guy whose house I was watchin' when I met Bianca."

"And what did you tell him?"

"I told him the truth. I found the house, but some shit went down over there, and now, I won't be able to go back."

"And what did he have to say about that?"

"He went off on me. Told me I was stupid as fuck for losin' focus. Whole lotta cuss words. Then, he hung up on me." Grizzy shrugged his massive shoulders. "Ain't shit I can do about it."

"Who is the man you're supposed to be watching?"

"Some nigga named Devonte Gibbs. They call him Butch."

Nya sucked her teeth and hung her mouth open in disbelief. "I wish you would've just told me that from the jump. I know him. He put a new roof on my mama's house last year. His daughter does my nails. I can call her right now."

A stunned expression appeared on Grizzy's face, and it remained there as Nya picked up her phone and dialed her manicurist's phone number.

While the phone rang on speaker, Nya shut her eyes and inhaled the soul-stirring scent of Grizzy's cologne. The liquor in her bloodstream had her buzzing in another dimension. She thought of the good time Lacey was probably having with Crunchy at this very moment and wished she could be in that same predicament with Grizzy. Nya was single, but she wasn't an all-out whore like her dear friend, Lacey. In the past six months, Nya had only had sex a dozen or so times, and with only three men. Lacey, on the other hand, had sex just about every day, sometimes with two or more men at once. Nya absolutely refused to even consider sex without protection, while Lacey fucked without protection on the regular and was always at the clinic trying to get rid of one STD or another. The two friends were polar opposites. At times, it seemed like Lacey was the one having all the fun, but that wasn't the case at all. Nya was the one who was always at peace, cooking in the kitchen, and cleaning up around the house while vibing to some good 90's R&B. Lacey was a perpetual source of relationship drama, always fighting over a man that wasn't hers to begin with.

Right now though, Nya had an overwhelming urge to act a little like Lacey. And why shouldn't she? Tomorrow was her twenty-first birthday. She had a fine-ass man sitting right beside her, a man with his own house, multiple vehicles, and the nuts to take care of his enemies like some sort of cowboy from the old west. She knew that she was rationalizing, mentally attempting to break down her usually impenetrable wall of defense for her own sexual pleasure, and she didn't feel a morsel of guilt about it either.

The phone call to Laporsha Gibbs, Nya's manicurist, went to voicemail, so she went to Laporsha's Facebook page and immediately understood why she hadn't gotten an answer. Laporsha was on Facebook Live, broadcasting live video and commentary of the shooting scene across the street from her Keystone Avenue home.

"...Like I said a few minutes ago, I didn't *see* the shooting go down. I was in the bathroom, getting dressed, when the gunshots started, but it sounded like a war zone..."

Laporsha was clearly filming from her upstairs bedroom window. The bodies of Mikey, Derrick, and their friend, Dre, were still stretched out on the sidewalk across the street. They were covered by white sheets that were saturated with blood. Yellow crime scene tape and CPD patrol cars blocked off the street at both ends. Little yellow pyramids with black numbers on them marked the places where all the shell casings had landed. A crowd of concerned neighbors and the distraught families of the victims were gathered behind the yellow tape, held back not by the tape itself but by the wall of uniformed policeman that stood on the other side of it.

Nya and Grizzy watched the video for several minutes without comment. Nya sipped from her drink. Grizzy rolled a blunt within a matter of seconds and put fire to one end of it while Nya dug around in her purse and dragged out her phone charger.

"I'll call her back in a little while," she said, scanning the room for the nearest power socket.

"You can just put your phone right there." Grizzy pointed at a flat section of the sofa on the other side of Nya. "That's a wireless charger. Just lay your phone on it and it'll start charging."

"Oh." Nya smiled a little. Turning on her knees to place her phone on the charging pad, she intentionally arched her back and wiggled her hips, and when Grizzy rewarded her with a sharp smack on the ass, her smile broadened, and she said, "Ouch! Bastard." She turned back around to face him, rubbing her stinging buttock. "You see I ain't got no ass as it is. You can't be smackin' on my lil cheeks like that. At least not until I get my BBL."

"You don't need no surgery, shorty. You got a nice lil handful back there. That's all you need." He blew out a plume of weed smoke and studied her smile through the dense haze of it.

Nya returned his gaze for a long while, lusting over his sexy lips and envisioning them slumped around her clitoris, wondering how his dick would look and feel in her hands, in her mouth, in her sopping-wet pussy. She looked down when she noticed the intimidating bulge in his jeans was returning, and throwing all caution to the wind, she reached for his Dior belt buckle. He didn't move as she undid the pin and snatched the bolt out of his belt loops.

"I just wanna see it," she said, lying more to herself than him.

Grizzy chuckled and assisted her by lifting up off the sofa, undoing his jeans, and pushing them down to his knees. The waistband of his black Burberry boxer briefs was red, matching his Dior shirt. His legs were nicely toned and only slightly hairy, and the print of his dick in the boxer briefs was even more intimidating than the bulge in his jeans had been.

"You can pull those down too," Nya said, pointing at the designer underwear, and she found herself holding her breath as his dick sprang free, and Nya's eyes became as wide and round as dinner plates. So did her mouth. She sucked in a breath on top of the one she'd been holding, and finally, after five, long seconds of ogling the astonishing girth and length of his erect, black phallus, she uttered a single word. "Wow."

She elongated the word, stretching it out for dramatic emphasis.

Then, she was digging around in her purse again, this time in search of her condoms. She knew she still had a half-empty box of ribbed Trojans and a fresh box of Magnums. This situation called for an extra-large Magnum.

But apparently, Grizzy had other plans because when Nya found the box of Magnums and looked back over her shoulder at him, he was pulling up his jeans and underwear and offering her the blunt.

"Uhhh, what are you doing?" she asked.

Grizzy stood up with his arm still extended toward Nya, the blunt pinched between his thumb and forefinger, sending wisps of smoke curling up toward the high ceiling. "You wanna hit this weed or not?"

Nya scowled at him and snatched the blunt from his fingers, eliciting an amused chuckle from the herculean man as he left her sitting there in the living room. She waited a few seconds and then got up to follow him. The brief pursuit ended in a large kitchen with smooth granite countertops and stainless-steel appliances. Grizzy pulled open the fridge and hunkered down to take a look inside it. Nya crossed her arms and puffed on the blunt.

"You're weird, dude," she said, nibbling at her thumbnail and barreling smoke out her nostrils.

"Weird? Because I don't wanna take advantage of an intoxicated twenty-year-old?"

"Whatever." Nya climbed onto one of the leather upholstered, barstool-like seats that ran along one side of the center island. "Whenever you're done doing whatever the fuck it is you're doing, I'd appreciate it if you took me home."

Another chuckle from Mr. Muscles. He rose from the fridge with a cold bottle of Bud Light in one hand. Walking over to the center island, he twisted the cap off his beer, drank from it, then sat it down on the island, and leaned forward, supporting himself with both hands.

"Thirty million dollars," he said.

Nya's brow came together in confusion.

"Thirty. Million. Dollars." He leaned in closer until his face and Nya's face were no more than twelve inches apart. "That's how much money Butch owes my pops. That's how much he was holding for my daddy when the Feds indicted the Stones in Altgeld Gardens. Pops just told me everything. Butch went down too, but he cooperated with the federal government and only ended up doing twelve years. When he got out, he went back to the Gardens. Somehow, word got out that he was a rat. Somebody shot his son, then his nephew got kidnapped and murdered. That's when he packed his shit and moved to the west side. Been laying low ever since."

Nya said nothing. Once again, she found herself at a loss for words. Thirty million dollars? Jesus Christ. That was enough money to take care of her entire family. All her friends too. And there was one thing she knew for certain. if she had $30 million in cash, there was no way in hell she'd still be living on the west side of Chicago.

"Butch ain't got no thirty million dollars," she said finally. "That man drives a fuckin' pickup truck. Millionaires don't drive pickup trucks. Not no Black millionaire at least."

"*Smart* Black millionaires do."

"No. Nuh uh. Butch ain't got no thirty million dollars. I'm telling you that now."

Nya wedged her thumbnail between her front teeth and thought it over. The weed was the kind of high-quality kush that always got her to thinking. She began pondering over Butch and his family's financial situation. His daughter, Lauren, was a hairstylist. LaPorsha was a manicurist. Both of them worked at Mariah's Salon just off Chicago Avenue and Central, which was right up the street and around the corner from where Nya lived. Butch's son, DT, was a highly skilled tattoo artist and also a full-time bouncer at The Visionary Lounge on Chicago Avenue and Laramie. Butch himself was a construction worker, and his wife was a high school teacher. They were regular people with regular jobs. Not millionaires.

"Looks can be deceiving," Grizzy said, picking up his beer. "Whatever the case, if you help me figure all this shit out and find that money, I'll cut you in on some of it." He came around to Nya's side of the island and sat down next to her, then he swiveled their seats, so they were facing each other.

"So, what the fuck do you want me to do?" Nya asked, coughing as she handed him the blunt.

"It's simple. If you're in, we go back over there tonight.in my Trackhawk. We kidnap Butch, and I'll torture him until he tells me where all that money is hidden. If you don't want nothin' to do with this shit, we can cut ties right now. I'll get you an Uber and send you on your way. Just promise to keep all this between me and you, and I'll never bother you again."

Nya stared into Grizzy's red-veined eyes as he raised the blunt to his lips and sucked in a mouthful of smoke. The liquor and marijuana mixture had her head spinning, but she was focused enough to make a conscientious decision. At least she believed she was.

"Okay, I'm in," she said, planting an elbow on the island's cool granite countertop to keep herself from toppling off the stool "But I think I have a much better idea than you going back over there yourself..."

Chapter 12

Devonte "Butch" Gibbs hadn't answered Johnna's first phone call and for good reason. He and two other construction carpenters had been busy all morning, building a wheelchair ramp for a beloved Vietnam war veteran who lived two doors down from the Gibbs' family home. They had just completed the job when the snake-like rattle of fully automatic gunfire sent them diving for cover, and now, the three men were standing around in Butch's fenced-in backyard, drinking beers and discussing the deadly shooting that had taken place across the street.

Butch was a fifty-seven-year-old former member of the Almighty Black P. Stones, and though he still bore the tattoos — a pyramid on his left pectoral muscle and a large, five-pointed star in the middle of his back with "A.B.P.S.N." arched across the top — he had put all that gang stuff behind him. Not that he'd had much of a choice. He'd gone against the code of the streets and helped the federal government bring down the entire faction of Stones that had controlled drug sales in Altgeld Gardens in the early 2000s, and now, many of his old friends wanted him dead.

Luckily for him, most of those old friends were serving federal prison sentences of four hundred fifty months or better. They wouldn't live to see the light of day. Meanwhile, Butch and his family were doing quite well. They had a nice home — in a questionable neighborhood but still a nice home — and none of them wanted for much. Butch owned a brand-new, 2023 Ford F250, the perfect vehicle for his line of work. His wife drove a 2023 Volkswagen Atlas. Their kids drove pre-owned vehicles, but they were low mileage, none older than three years. The Gibbs were doing just fine, and despite the recent spike in gun violence that had most law-abiding families in their community on edge, their home felt to them like the safest place on Earth.

The two-story, red brick building consisted of three separate apartments - a three-bedroom on the first floor, a three-bedroom on the second floor, and a two-bedroom in the basement. Butch and his wife, Monique, lived on the first floor with her seventy-two-year-old mother, Gloria, and their three-year-old French bulldog, White Moe. Their daughters, Lauren and LaPorsha, ages thirty and twenty-eight, shared the second-floor apartment with Lauren's boyfriend, Ray. Their twenty-year-old son, DJ, and his girlfriend, Ariel, lived in the basement apartment. DJ had converted the spare bedroom into a tattoo studio, and there was always a list of people willing to pay top dollar to get their tattoos done by him.

Butch owned the entire building.

In fact, Butch owned nearly every property on the block. He'd purchased them through a shell company, a trick he'd learned from a white-collar criminal mastermind during his stint in federal prison. He'd managed to keep the gang violence on Thomas and Keystone to a minimum in recent years by buying up the properties and primarily renting to seniors and women whose spouses and adult children had no criminal records or gang affiliations. He'd tried multiple times to purchase the house directly across the street from his own home, where today's shooting had taken place, as well as the house farther up the street where the boys who were killed had lived, but the owners weren't budging.

No one but his wife knew the full extent of Butch's real estate portfolio. The kids were currently under the impression that they'd only be inheriting the house they lived in. Altogether, Butch owned the deeds to seventeen properties, and he was in the process of paying off the fifteen-year mortgages on eleven more, one of which was the fifteen-acre ranch in Amarillo, Texas where he and his wife planned to retire in the spring of 2025.

The time on Butch's Timex wristwatch was 2:32 p.m. when he said his goodbyes to Jack and Leron, two of the first men he'd hired to work alongside him at Butch's Roofing and Renovation, LLC. He now had forty-three full-time employees on his payroll and was averaging $38,500 a month in what he liked to call "after work income", which was essentially the profit he deposited into his personal checking account every month after paying his employees and all the annoying but necessary expenses that came with running a successful construction business.

Jack's pickup truck was parked in the alleyway behind the veteran's house, so he and Leron had no trouble leaving the area. They'd have been fucked had they parked out front where about fifty Chicago police officers were busy securing the scene.

When Butch walked in the back door of his house, he found Monique standing there beside the kitchen table with her fists on her hips and a troubled expression on her pudgy, brown face. She had obviously been waiting for him to come inside. His iPhone was on the table next to her vastly sloping hip (he could tell the phone was his because of the crack at the top right-hand corner of the screen), and for a second, he thought she might have gone through it and found evidence of the affair he'd been having with Jack's wife.

"Guess who called you while you and the boys were out there working on old Jeff Hatfield's wheelchair ramp," she said, picking up the phone. "Take a wild guess."

He shrugged. "Fuck if I know. Who was it?"

She walked over and handed him the phone, and her fists made a swift return to her hips. She was a full-figured woman in a shimmery gold Alexander McQueen jumpsuit and four-inch Jimmy Choo heels. Lauren had whipped her hair up in a complicated wrap with a bang that hung down over the left side of her forehead. Her fingernails were stiletto-tipped, black with glittery golden stars, and professionally done by LaPorsha.

Butch loved his wife's sense of fashion almost more than he loved her every curve.

He unlocked the phone screen, went to the missed calls, and was surprised to see that Panteon Tech CEO Johnna Broward had called him a short while ago. Johnna Broward was a conniving little woman who had taken his dick down her throat and deep in her asshole just so she could put him to sleep and rob him of his ill-gotten fortune. The memory of that regretful night in Amarillo four years ago still haunted him to this day. Ever since then, he'd been a lot more careful with the women he dealt with outside of his marriage. Never again would he boast about his fortune to impress a potential mistress, and he most certainly wouldn't be taking another woman to his ranch. That torrid, two-week affair with Johnna Broward had taught him a valuable lesson.

When he looked up from his phone, Monique had already turned around and was walking off toward the living room.

"Come and see this," she said, "and you'll see why she called you."

Butch was all too happy to shadow his wife into the living room, if only to gaze at her massive derriere as she walked ahead of him. Butch was a scrawny wisp of a man, six feet even and a hundred sixty pounds on his heaviest day. He'd been lanky all his life, and he'd always had a thing for women with a lot of fat on their bones — especially when that fat protruded from their backsides.

When they reached the living room, Monique gestured toward their seventy-inch smart TV. MTN News was on *Today with Alexandria Ray*. The caption at the bottom of the screen read: EIGHT SHOT, FIVE KILLED PANTEON TECH HQ SHOOTING. The television was muted, but the

STEPPERS | KING RIO

close captioning was on. Butch only needed to read a few sentences to understand Johnna's reason for phoning him.

Michael Caldwell, the only other co-defendant in that infamous forty-nine count indictment against the Black P. Stones from Altgeld Gardens, who had cooperated with the government in exchange for a more lenient sentence, had gone on a shooting-spree inside Panteon Tech, killing four and wounding three others before he was fatally wounded by a newly hired security guard. Caldwell had reportedly assaulted Johnna Broward just before he was shot and killed.

And Butch knew exactly why Caldwell had done it. In a way, Butch had put him up to it.

"She got exactly what she deserved," Monique said snappily. "God don't like ugly, and He just proved it. Karma came back around and hit Johnna on that big ol' fake ass she paid an arm and a leg for. I hate to say it, but I wish he would've killed her ass."

"I'm the one who talked her into hiring Mike," Butch said, picking a wood chip off his forearm. "I sent her about ten or fifteen emails about it."

"Good. I'm glad you did it too."

"I only did it to get the nigga away from us. He kept inboxin' me on Facebook, askin' me about the money. I ain't want him tryna find out where we live, so I told him what happened to the money and where he might be able to find it, then I started emailing Johnna about hiring him. Told her he was a solid guy who really needed a job, that it was the least she could do after what she did to us."

Monique shook her head and continued to stare at the TV. Her normally welcoming expression had morphed into a mask of intense displeasure. A bead of sweat trickled out of a crease in her neck. From the side, her fat ass stuck out as if she was attempting to conceal a beach ball in her jumpsuit. Butch's dick twitched in response to the arousing view of it. He stepped around the tan, leather sofa and headed for the bathroom, knowing his wife wouldn't be far behind him.

And he was right. He had started the shower and was peeling off his work clothes when Monique entered the bathroom and pushed the door shut behind her.

"You do plan on calling her back, right?"

"I hate that woman," Butch said, and he really meant it.

He spent a few seconds studying his reflection in the large, oval mirror above the sink. He had a pecan-brown complexion and a narrow bald head with a neatly trimmed mustache that circled around to the bottom of his mouth and connected to an equally well-groomed goatee. His eyes had grown dull with age and were wrinkled at the corners. He was somewhat handsome, but he was growing old. Almost sixty. Had Johnna not stolen all that money, he'd have almost certainly retired by now.

Taking off his underwear and stepping into the shower, he said, "If I call Johnna, the only thing I'ma end up doin' is cussin' her out."

"No," Monique said. "You're gonna call her back. You're gonna call her back and tell her that if she doesn't pay back what she stole from us, the next time someone walks into her office with a gun, security won't be able to save her."

Butch didn't reply. He squeezed a dollop of Old Spice body wash onto a loofah and began scrubbing himself clean, all the while thinking over the situation with Johnna. He had a general idea of why she had called him. He'd suggested she hire Michael Caldwell, and three months later, Caldwell had gone ballistic. Was she only calling to tell him about it? Was she upset with him for convincing her to hire Caldwell in the first place? Had the shooting put her in some sort of vulnerable state of mind, one that might compel her to return the millions of dollars she'd stolen from him?

"We've got to at least *try* to get the money back," Monique said. She sounded oddly defeated. "We can't just give up and let her win like this. She's a fucking billionaire. She can more than afford it."

66

"I agree, baby," Butch said, absentmindedly stroking his dick in one hand while he scrubbed his chest with the loofah.

"We can't stay in this neighborhood much longer, Butch. Buying up every house on the block isn't going to change the fact that it's not safe here. A triple-murder just went down right across the street from our house. Our best move right now is to force Johnna's hand, get her to give us that money back, and get the fuck out of Chicago before the shit *really* hits the fan."

Chapter 13

Four blacked-out Escalades pulled up beside Johnna's Gulfstream jet as soon as it landed at O'Hare, and soon, she and Jayvon were in the backseat of one of them, lancing away from the airport in a motorcade fit for a high-level government official.

Figuring enough time had passed since the shooting to share something with her millions of followers, Johnna composed a brief message and posted it to her Instagram page. It was just three words, Pray for Panteon, followed by brown prayer hands and a broken heart emoji. She shared it to Facebook as well, and within minutes, the poignant post was liked by more than a million people.

She sat her phone on her lap and looked over at Jayvon. He still had on the black tee shirt with SECURITY emblazoned across the back in large yellow and black letters. A smaller version of the word graced the left side chest area. His big, black beard partially obscured the first four letters of the word as he turned and gazed down at her.

"You okay, Ms. Broward?" Jayvon asked, his deep voice sending chills through Johnna's diminutive, little body.

Johnna nodded her head somberly, exhaled a dramatic sigh, and reached over to place her head in the palm of his, interlacing their fingers. Her hand was like a child's hand in his mammoth paw.

"Thank you so much," she said. "I don't know how I could ever repay you. That man would have killed me had you not shown up when you did. You're a hero, Jayvon. A real-life hero."

She raised their interlocked hands, swiveled her wrist so that his arm was on top of hers, and planted a delicate kiss on the back of his hand before lowering their arms back down onto the armrest between them. He smiled appreciatively and said nothing, and for a while, they rode in silence. Her driver was taking them to her high-rise condominium, a two-story penthouse that took up the top two floors in a luxury Streetersville apartment building overlooking Lake Shore Drive.

After a time, Jayvon said, "I was only doing my job."

"And you did, Jayvon. You did it well."

The warmth of his hand against hers made Johnna's heart skip a beat. She could feel her vaginal juices burgeoning within her, becoming more and more plentiful. Her mouth began to water. Her breathing hastened. She was gathering the courage to take the leap she'd been preparing herself to take ever since she first hired Jayvon three days ago.

There was a black, leather-upholstered wall spanning the length of the seats in front of them. Inside the wall was a tinted glass partition. Using her free hand, Johnna reached over to her door and pressed the button that raised the partition, giving her and Jayvon complete privacy.

Something in him must have sensed her lascivious intentions because, suddenly, he was squeezing her hand and looking over at her with those warm, brown eyes of his. Her lungs inflated with a breath that she held for an unreasonable amount of time. She felt her heart beating — *thump-thump, thump-thump* — in her chest. Her Apple wristwatch informed her that her heart rate had increased significantly.

"Jayvon," she said, her nervous gaze locked on their coupled hands. "I, um… I really like you. I mean, I know your situation, and I know it's not right to say this, with you having a wife and a kid at home, but…"

She didn't get it all out. Jayvon took her chin in his hand, tilted her face toward his, and moved in for a kiss. Johnna fell into it, freeing her hand from his grasp to cradle the sides of his face as she kissed him repeatedly, impervious to the stinging ache she felt where the laceration in her lip was sutured. She climbed over the armrest and settled onto his lap, grinding her pelvis onto his crotch. His oversized hands squeezed and caressed the fat bouncy butt cheeks she'd paid Dr. Miami $10,500 to surgically enlarge and sculpt to perfection.

When their lips separated a moment later, she lifted his tee shirt over his head and threw it aside. Then, she made the bold decision to undo his black, leather belt and his clean black slacks and free his raging hard member. It was hot and fat and throbbing in her hand, maybe eight inches in length, and Johnna couldn't get it inside of her fast enough.

She maneuvered her way out of her skintight leggings, kicking off her expensive designer sneakers in the process. Johnna never wore underwear, so she was immediately able to lower herself onto the bulbous head of his erection. He sank his fingers into the soft flesh of her ass as she skewered herself on his rigid pole. Eager to fully impale her, he pulled on her ass until he was just about balls deep in her gushy center, and then, she was going up and down, kissing him, holding onto his shoulders, and throwing her head back and panting with her mouth open wide as the girth of his dick stretched her to the limit.

Johnna cast a victorious smile at the ceiling as she marveled over all she'd done. Her big brother, Johnny, had always taught her to be a taker, and that was precisely what she'd become. When Johnny told her about Butch and the $30 million he'd essentially stolen from the Black P. Stones, she'd used her stunning looks and mouthwatering curves to reel him into a plot that could have gained a Hollywood screenwriter an Academy Award. She'd talked him into taking her to his $700,000 north Texas ranch and showing her the suitcases full of cash he had piled up in a spare bedroom, and after a wild night of raucous sex and hard drinks, she'd sat beside him in bed, watching him sleep, while a team of professional movers loaded seventy-one cash filled suitcases into a U-Haul truck she'd rented exclusively for the occasion. To this day, Butch still didn't know that she'd actually crushed up a bunch of Melatonin and mixed them in with his cognac before they started fucking that night. She'd outsmarted him and made off with $23 million in drug money.

And now, she had taken again. She'd stalked Jayvon on social media, reeled him in with an irresistible job offer, and got him right where she'd wanted him from the start. She'd taken Estrella's husband the same way she'd taken Butch's millions — by outsmarting her prey. She was the undisputed queen of the jungle, the lioness who went out and took what she needed from the animal kingdom, the young, Black female billionaire who'd started her company with the $23 million she'd taken from a former member of one of Chicago's most notorious street gangs, and no one was going to stop her.

"Put it in my ass," she said, moving off of Jayvon and raising the armrest, so she could kneel on the seat with her ass up and her back arched seductively before him.

He did as she asked, slowly easing himself into her asshole. It was exactly what Johnna needed to push her over the edge. She let out a high-pitched yelp and began furiously massaging her clitoris, and Jayvon closed his strong hands around her trembling waist and continued to piston in and out of her as her vaginal juices rained down onto the rich, black, leather seat below.

Chapter 14

Lacey was in one of her moods.

She had showered and changed into an all-black ensemble of Air Force One sneakers, Palm Angels sweatpants, and a tee shirt with a phone on the front that showed Rihanna holding up two middle fingers.

The shirt summed up Lacey's mood quite perfectly. She had called Crunchy's phone twenty-three times in a row, and he hadn't answered once. She'd texted him seventeen times, and he had yet to reply. And to make matters worse, she'd tried calling him a twenty-fourth time, only to learn that she'd been blocked.

Now she sat fuming on the living room sofa, watching an episode of *Karamo* without really watching it at all. It was one of her favorite shows, but right now, all she could think about was busting Crunchy upside his goddamn head. Maybe she'd split that awful unibrow in two. Do the whole world a favor. Not being able to confront Crunchy about the money he'd stolen off her dresser was really starting to get to Lacey. She sat silently on the sofa with her shoe tapping out a morse code on the floor until, finally, in a blazing hot fit of rage, she snatched her phone off the coffee table and went live on Instagram to let all 27,942 of her followers know exactly how she was feeling about Tyreoun "Crunchy" Pinkston.

"How a nigga with one long ass eyebrow gon' try to play me?" Lacey started. "I mean, for real. This *bum* ass nigga gave me a thousand dollars, ate my pussy, and then stole the money back before he left. Ol' broke-ass nigga. Ol' crackhead lookin', meth smokin', skinny dick havin', weak ass nigga. Bitch bett' not *never* say another word to me. On my dead grandmama. Punk ass nigga damn near pissed himself when Cold Gang called him with all them guns out. That's why Cold Gang on yo' ass, Crunchy! You's a bitch-ass nigga, Tyreoun Pinkston!"

Lacey took a short break from her enraged monologue to relight the blunt she'd rolled a few minutes earlier and read the comments that were already starting to pop up on her phone screen.

"Somebody get Lacey."

"Girl, who done pissed you off?"

"Cold Gang and Wicked Town beefin' now?"

"Lmaooooo!! Tooo funny."

"Crunchy got $1,000? That nigga still owe me $70 from before Christmas."

The last comment had come from LaPorsha Gibbs, a makeup artist and manicurist at Mariah's Salon, who had dated Crunchy on and off for the past few years. Seeing the comment from LaPorsha made Lacey think of Butch, LaPorsha's father. The horny, old man was always flirting with her, telling her how beautiful he thought she looked and offering her rides whenever he saw her walking the neighborhood. A few days ago, she'd let him give her a ride to the CVS drug store on Pulaski, and he'd offered her a crisp, new, fifty-dollar bill for a blow job. She'd needed the money, and she'd always considered Butch to be a bit on the handsome side, so she'd sucked him off while they waited in the CVS parking lot for her Percocet prescription to be filled.

"Hey, LaPorsha," Lacey said, a sudden smile on her face. "Yeah, that bum ass nigga got a thousand dollars. Matter fact, he got *five* thousand dollars, so you need to find his crackhead ass before he trick it all off on the next bitch he put his tongue all in and tell yo' daddy I said heyyy."

The livestream was up to twelve thousand viewers and counting. Many of them weren't even Lacey's followers. She continued her profanity laced rant against Crunchy for a short while longer. She brought up the time he'd been stabbed and knocked unconscious while serving time in Cook County Jail's notoriously ruthless "Division 9." She mentioned the time he'd asked her to lick his asshole while he jerked off and how she'd cussed him out for even asking her some disgusting shit like that.

The viewership had just risen past twenty-thousand, and the comments (mostly laughing emojis) were pouring in when Lacey decided she'd said enough and ended the livestream. Feeling relieved, she puffed on the remainder of her blunt and connected her phone to the charger.

Five seconds later, the front door behind her was kicked in.

She lunged to the right — away from the splintering doorway — and screamed. She turned toward the door but only managed to get a fleeting glimpse of two intruders with ski masks on their heads before one of the men grabbed her by the hair and shoved her face toward the floor. She felt something hard, cold, and metallic being pressed against her ear and immediately knew it was a pistol.

"Where Nya at with that one nigga?!" the man screamed aggressively.

His voice was unmistakably familiar.

It was Crunchy.

Chapter 15

"I... I d-don't know," Lacey stuttered, leaning into Crunchy's grasp on her hair to reduce the pain as he held his .45 caliber Glock 30 to the other side of her head.

Crunchy looked back at his younger brother, Kion "Curry" Pinkston. He was busy trying to lift the heavy wooden door up on its broken hinges to push it shut. Curry had gotten his nickname not only because he was known for toting guns with thirty shot clips — like the "30" Golden State Warriors star Steph Curry wore on his jersey — but also because he very rarely missed his target when he took aim at an opposing gang member.

Returning his attention to Lacey, Crunchy threw her back onto the sectional sofa and stood over her with his Glock aimed at her face. He wasn't here because of her incessant phone calls and text messages or because of her attempts to embarrass him on Instagram. In fact, he didn't even know about any of that. He'd left his phone at home with his sister, Brittney, and he had no idea that she'd grown tired of Lacey's calls and blocked her.

He and Curry had intentionally left their phones behind, so the police wouldn't be able to track their movements if they ended up having to murder someone.

Charles "Wobble" Dawkins, the longtime leader of the Wicked Town TVLs, had spoken with Sleet, the leader of the Cold Gang CVLs, shortly after receiving news of their issue with Crunchy. He'd offered Sleet Crunchy's version of events, that Crunchy had only given the man called Renzo a ride in the stolen Altima and then sold it to him for $5,000 and that he had chosen to stay with Lacey when Nya and Renzo left in the Altima. But Sleet wasn't trying to hear it. He'd demanded some sort of retribution. If Crunchy couldn't locate the man to whom he'd sold the car to within the next twenty-four hours, then Cold Gang would take it out on Crunchy and his family — and whoever else wanted to get involved. In an effort to avoid war with one of the most dominant street gangs in the city, Wobble had ordered Crunchy and Curry to do whatever they could to track down Nya and Renzo, and in the meantime, the other Wicked Town Ts would be gearing up for war.

Crunchy took a seat on the aged wooden coffee table and stared at Lacey through the eyeholes of his mask. "Get on that phone and call Nya," he said, speaking authoritatively.

Lacey appeared frightened, flicking her eyes back-and-forth between the two brothers, but Crunchy kept his Glock trained on the center of her chest. He had to. She was taller than both him and Curry, and she outweighed them both by at least a hundred pounds. She was also a wild girl who knew how to throw her weight around. She'd nearly choked Crunchy out during a heated argument once, and he knew of at least three grown men she'd defeated in actual fist fights in front of everyone in the neighborhood. Not to mention, all the girls she'd beaten unconscious over the years.

She reached for her phone with one trembling hand. "Crunchy, why are you doing this? It ain't even that deep. Fuck that thousand dollars. You can have that shit."

Crunchy rolled his black, cotton ski mask up to his unibrow. "This ain't got shit to do with that thousand dollars. I took that money 'cause I'ma need it to deal with them Cold Gang niggas. Guns, bullets, a whip — I'ma need all that shit. All this shit started when Nya lied and said that nigga was her boyfriend. I ain't about to lose none of my people over this bullshit, and I definitely ain't tryna lose my life or take somebody else's over some shit I ain't have nothing to do with. So, get on that phone, call Nya, and find out where Renzo at. You do that and we'll be outta here, and I'll pay for that door *and* give you that thousand dollars back."

Curry walked off to search the rest of the house, holding his P90 Ruger low in both hands like a trained policeman. He was only seventeen years old, and he'd already shot six rival gang members, one of them on two separate occasions. He had yet to take a life, but he'd put one in a wheelchair, paralyzed from the waist down, and he'd left another rival with permanent brain damage.

Lacey dialed a number and put the call on speaker, and as the line began to ring, Crunchy reached up to pull his mask back down over his face.

In the split second that the rolled portion of his mask passed over his eyes, he glimpsed a lightning-fast blur. Something hard crashed into his jaw, and his world went black.

When he came to, the first thing he sensed was the coppery taste of blood in his mouth. Then, he realized his breathing was restricted and that there was an arm wrapped around the front of his neck, holding him up. Curry was standing about six feet ahead of him. It seemed like Curry's P90 was aimed directly at Crunchy's face.

"Bruh, what the fuck…" Crunchy croaked. Then, he felt the barrel of a gun at his temple, and a few seconds later, he figured it all out. Somehow, Lacey had been able to knock him unconscious and disarm him, and now, she'd turned the tables.

"Go ahead and shoot, Curry," she goaded. "I know that's you under there. Go on and pull that trigger. You shoot me, I shoot him, and we'll both be dead. Fuck it. Let's do it."

"Come on now, Bigfoot. Don't make me fire yo' big ass up," Curry warned.

"Either you put that gun down and get the fuck out my house or I'm about to blow this skinny bitch's brains all over that coffee table. Now, what it's gon' be?"

Crunchy raised his hand palm out at his younger brother, like a crossing guard trying to stop a vehicle from continuing forward so a group of school children could get across the street.

"Lil bruh," he said, "just listen to her. Put it down. She ain't gon' shoot you."

He found it difficult to speak. There was blood pouring out of his mouth, and he had the distinct feeling that his jaw was broken.

If this big bitch done broke my jaw, he thought, *I'ma kill her my goddamn self.*

Chapter 16

Nya sat staring at her phone with her eyes wide and her heart pounding. She looked over at Grizzy, but he didn't return her gaze. His eyes were on the road ahead, his right hand closed around the wood of his steering wheel as they raced down Interstate 290 in his Jeep Grand Cherokee Trailhawk, commonly referred to as a Trackhawk.

The SUV was as fast as a muscle car, and it sounded like one too. Two of Grizzy's boys were in the backseat with miniature assault rifles on their laps, listening silently to the showdown that was currently taking place at Nya and Lacey's house. The two men were Gangster Disciples they'd picked up from the corner of 78th and Paulina in the Auburn Gresham neighborhood. Grizzy's Uncle Titus was a governor for the GDs in that area, and he'd given Grizzy a drug spot in the apartment building located at 1651 West 78th Street. The two men were called Smoke and Uptown. Grizzy's cousin, Marcus, and two more GDs were trailing the Trackhawk in a dark green Dodge Charger Hellcat.

It had been Nya's idea to bring the others. Grizzy had wanted to go after Butch on his own, but even in her halfway intoxicated state, Nya understood that it wasn't wise for Grizzy to be returning to the Keystone Avenue area after having committed a triple homicide there hours earlier. Sure, he'd had most of his face covered during the shooting, and he'd changed into a black Amiri jogger before they left his house, but the fact remained that Mikey's crew had seen his face when they carjacked him. Nya was almost certain that the two men she'd seen pointing guns at Grizzy as they jacked his Escalade were Derrick and Mikey, but if that wasn't the case, then who was driving Mikey's Durango?

And who was in that white Tahoe?

Grizzy's Escalade had been found ablaze in a vacant lot somewhere in the South Lawndale neighborhood. Nya had eavesdropped on Grizzy's half of the conversation when someone called to tell him about it. At the time, it had seemed like good news, brightening her mood, but now, as she listened to what sounded like an armed standoff in her own home, Nya's mood was anything but bright.

"Put the gun down right there on the floor," Lacey was saying. "I'm serious, Curry. I'll blow his fuckin' dreads off. Put it down and I'll let both of y'all walk outta here. *Don't* put it down and see how fast I pull this motherfuckin' trigger."

A tense moment of nothing ensued, then, croakily, "Bruh, just listen to her." It was Crunchy's voice, but again, it sounded raspy, as if he'd just awakened from a deep slumber. In Nya's mind, she could see Lacey's long, brown arm coiled around the front of Crunchy's neck, restraining him in a sleeper hold while holding a gun to his head.

"A'ight, a'ight," Crunchy's younger brother said, and two seconds later, there was a solid clunking sound. "There. Now let him go."

A sudden rattle of fully automatic gunfire sent Nya cringing against the back of her seat, and over the next minute or so, as she and the others in the Trackhawk sat listening to the frantic overlapping voices of Lacey, Crunchy, and Curry, she was able to make out what had happened. Lacey had intentionally shot Curry in the leg, so Crunchy would have to worry about getting him to a hospital instead of retaliating against her for holding them at gunpoint, but she hadn't anticipated the gun being modified with a Glock switch, and instead of one shot, she'd fired many, striking Curry multiple times.

The tense situation, exacerbated by the blunt of Kush she'd smoked with Grizzy, drove Nya to a state of paranoia, and she hurriedly ended the phone call.

"What in the world..." she said in fluctuating tones of bewilderment.

Uptown sat forward. "Damn, shorty. It's crackin' like that at 'cho crib?"

Nya didn't utter a single syllable. Neither did Grizzy. They had just left the interstate and were on Central Avenue, darting through traffic toward the house where apparently all hell had just broken loose.

Nya's eyes wandered down to her purse. It was beside her hip, and inside it was the Glock 27 Grizzy had taken from one of the boys on Keystone. He'd reloaded the extended magazine right in front of her, so she knew there were twenty-nine rounds in the clip and one in the chamber. They were nine-millimeter bullets with some sort of blue coating at the tips. He'd sold the modified Glock he had used to gun down Mikey, Derrick, and Dre, and now, he had a 7.62-millimeter Mini Draco pistol on his lap. The Draco had an enormous double-drum magazine, the kind boys in Nya's neighborhood called "monkey nuts."

Three minutes after Nya had ended the call, Lacey called back.

"I just ran down to Briella's house," she said, sounding out of breath. "Nya, do *not* come over here. We can meet up somewhere else, just not around here. They told Cold Gang about you and ol' boy. I guess Wicket Town sent Crunchy and Curry back over here to try and force me to tell them where y'all went."

"Where did Crunchy and Curry go?"

"Crunchy helped him into a Lumina. Like a silver-colored Chevy Lumina. I'm about to call the police and report this shit, so I don't get fucked around. I can't go to no jail, Nya.

STEPPERS | KING RIO

I'm too pretty for all that shit. I'll be done strangled one of them bull dyke bitches."

"No, Lacey," Nya said with a short chuckle. "No police. Just sit still. Did you lock up the house?"

"They kicked the fuckin' door in, Nya. Ain't no more lockin' that front door. It's hangin' off the hinges. I took their guns, and I took that whole five Gs outta Crunchy's pocket when I knocked him out, but they could be coming back at any minute. I think I shot Curry about six or seven times in his legs."

Nya paused, holding the tip of her thumbnail between her front teeth. "It'll be fine," she said finally. "Just sit there and chill. You can keep an eye on the house from Brielle's living room window. But don't call the police. And don't tell nobody else. I'll call you back in a few minutes."

She ended the call and sighed just as they were riding past her house. The front door had clearly been kicked in. There was a shoeprint just below the doorknob, and the door itself hung awkwardly on its one remaining hinge. A trail of blood stretched from the doorway, down the concrete porch steps, and all the way to the curb.

Turning to look across the street at Brielle's house, she caught a fleeting glimpse of Lacey peeking out through the blinds. Brielle's three-year-old daughter, Brenique, was right there beside Lacey, her Black, little fingers weighing down on the blinds and exposing her and Lacey to anyone looking their way.

Grizzy slowed the Trackhawk as they approached the intersection of Chicago Avenue and Central. A blue Dodge Challenger Hellcat rounded the corner off of Chicago Avenue and cruised past them. Nya held her breath and turned in her seat to watch the clean, blue muscle car as it rolled slowly toward her house. The car had tinted windows, and Nya had only gotten a quick look. Through the front windshield, she'd seen two, young, Black men, both of them with dreadlocks, and she didn't recognize either of them.

Nya had a horrible gut feeling that whoever was in that Hellcat was up to no good.

"There go twelve, y'all. Be cool," Grizzy muttered nervously as he braked to a stop at the red light.

Nya flicked her bloodshot eyes back to the intersection and sucked in another breath when she spotted the CPD Tahoe. It was turning the corner, heading in the same direction as the blue Challenger Hellcat. There were white policemen inside it, and two of them looked in at Grizzy and Nya before shifting their attention to a group of Black male teenagers who were just exiting the convenience store at the corner.

Nya swiveled in her seat to look back at the Challenger — just as the short barrels of two Dracos were pushed out of its passenger's side windows.

The gunfire was deafening. Nya gasped as she realized the shooters were targeting her house. The CPD Tahoe's light and sirens came on almost instantly, and the Hellcat's tires screeched and smoked as it shot off down Central Avenue.

"Goddamn, lil mama," Uptown said as he and Smoke twisted around in their seats to peer out the tinted back window. "What the fuck you done got yo'self into?"

Nya was thinking the same thing, and then, the Challenger Hellcat crashed into a parked Hyundai about a block and a half back, and her mind went blank as she watched its passenger's side doors swing open. Two slim boys staggered out with Dracos in hand. The CPD Tahoe screeched to a halt, and the three cops leapt into action, jumping out with their guns raised and aimed at the armed young men.

"Drop your weapons!" one cop yelled.

"We'll fucking shoot!" shouted another.

Grizzy hit the gas and careened onto Chicago Avenue half a second before the barrage of gunfire began.

Chapter 17

"Turn that up," Johnna said, looking up from her phone to watch her legendary attorney, Nikkia Staples, work her magic on CNN's *The Situation Room with Wolf Blitzer.*

Jayvon picked up the remote and pressed down on the volume increase button until the surround sound was at a reasonably loud forty-two. His right arm was long and thick with muscles. On his forearm was a tattoo of an apartment building with the words "Brownsville Projects" and "R.I.P. Azar Supreme" inked below it.

"Johnna is, quite honestly, the strongest Black woman I know besides my good friend, Alexus Costilla," Nikkia was saying. "To have survived something like this will undoubtedly result in some sort of trauma, and she'll almost certainly need some counseling to deal with that trauma, but trust and believe me when I say that Johnna Broward will emerge from this terrible situation much stronger than she was before."

"That's Alexus Costilla's lawyer," Jayvon said matter-of-factly.

Johnna nodded her head and lowered her eyes back to her phone screen. She was messaging her team of Panteon executives on a group chat they'd had for a couple of years now. Everyone was worried about the lawsuits that were surely coming their way. Tabitha Green's family had already hired an attorney.

The white, Italian, leather sofas and chairs in the living room of Johnna's forty-million-dollar, Streeterville penthouse were weighed down by the asses of six of her closest friends and family members. Among them were her younger sisters, Johnesha and Johnetta, her mother, April, and her mother's mother, Gwendolyn, all of them dressed in high-end designer duds like a ghetto family that had recently won the Mega Millions jackpot. Johnna's childhood friends from Altgeld Gardens, Pandy and Cherrelle, were also present. They hadn't asked Johnna many questions about the shooting, but they were all watching the news coverage on her one hundred twenty-inch 4KHD TV screen and talking about it amongst themselves — anything to avoid asking the questions they *really* wanted to ask, questions about the fine young man who was sitting beside Johnna with one arm extended behind her.

Johnna was just about finished composing a text message to her business partners when her phone buzzed with an incoming FaceTime call from Butch. A small smile lifted one corner of her mouth, and she got up from the sofa and slipped her bare feet into her new pair of Gucci slides. She had showered after arriving at the 9,200 square foot penthouse and put on a white Gucci bathrobe over a red, lace Savage X Fenty bra, and she had swallowed two thirty milligram Percocets to soothe her tattered mind.

She put in an AirPod Pro wireless earbud and started up the glass butterfly staircase to her master bedroom as she answered the call. When Butch's face appeared on her phone screen, she looked down and regarded him with her most innocent smirk.

"I want my fuckin' money, Johnna. All twenty-three million dollars of it plus interest. I'm done playin' these fuckin' reindeer games with you," he barked angrily.

"I could have lost my life earlier today, and this is the kind of treatment I get from you?"

"Next time, you will lose it. I can guarantee you that."

Johnna paused on the clear glass steps and stared coldly at the man on her phone screen. He was outside somewhere; she could see a tall, wooden fence and trees in the background. A small brown bird landed on the fence, just over his shoulder, chirped a couple of times, and then took to the air. There were also voices somewhere in the distance and the distinctive sound of police radios.

Johnna hesitated.

Was Butch trying to set her up? Had he gone back to working with the FBI?

"What's all that noise I hear?" Johnna asked, continuing up the staircase.

"What the fuck it sound like? It's the police. Five muthafuckas got shot right across the street from my house a few hours ago. Three of em died. You'd have thought Willie White and that psychotic-ass brother of yours was back out here. That's why I need my goddamn money. So, I can pack my shit and get the fuck outta Dodge."

"Hold on a second, Butch."

Johnna reached the top of the staircase, breezed past a Hispanic maid, who was busy mopping the gray-veined, white, marble floor, and then entered her massive master bedroom and pushed the heavy oak door shut behind her. She went to the wall of floor to ceiling windows and pulled back the white, silk curtains to gaze out over the rolling blue waters of Lake Michigan then raised her phone to address Butch in private.

"First of all," she said, "that money was never yours to begin with. It belonged to Willie White, the leader of the Black P. Stones I just so happened to grow up around. My big brother, Johnny, was Willie White's right-hand man. That money was just as much his as it was yours. And…"

"Who did you *get* the money from? Huh? Who did you *steal* it from?"

"*And secondly*," she said, talking over him, "I've given you some of that money back. Are you forgetting that? I've sent you more than a million dollars over the past few years, legitimate money that you could have used to buy any-fucking-thing you wanted. You're the one who chose to buy up a bunch of properties in the middle of the ghetto. That's on you."

"*BITCH!* Are you fuckin' serious? You stole twenty-three *million* from me. What the fuck is a million dollars? You stole twenty-three million dollars of my money and used it to become a goddamn billionaire. A *billionaire.* You could send me fifty million right now and not lose a wink of sleep. I saw on some website a few months ago that you bought a fifty-million-dollar mansion in The Hamptons and that you already owned a forty-million-dollar condo right here in Chicago and another one somewhere in New York."

"What does that have to do with anything? I bought all that with money I made from Panteon Technologies."

"There wouldn't *be* a Panteon Technologies if you hadn't stolen my fuckin' money!"

"And you'd *have* some money had you not gambled away over three million dollars in Vegas and another eight hundred thousand at The Bunny Ranch. And Lord knows how much more you've blown on drugs and alcohol and that sick fucking sex addiction you have. You did tell me about that, remember? Or were you too high that night?"

Johnna closed the curtain and crossed the room to sit on her California King bed. She'd never admit it, especially to Butch, but Michael Caldwell had frightened her half to death when he barged into her office with that smoking rifle in his hand. If Butch had intentionally sent him on that killing spree, then what else was he capable of doing?

One thing was clear. Johnna could no longer afford to keep playing around with Butch. Something had to give. If she didn't do something soon, her entire business could end up going down the drain, right along with her net worth. If word ever got out that she'd financed Panteon with $22 million worth of some incarcerated gang leader's illicit drug money, investors would start pulling out left and right, and Panteon stocks would plummet. Either she was going to have to pay Butch the money she owed him, or she was going to have to pay someone else to get rid of him.

The latter option was clearly the cheaper of the two. Plus, how would it look if she sent a former Black P. Stone from Altgeld Gardens millions of dollars when a former member of the same gang had just murdered four of her employees? It would look like she'd *planned* the workplace shooting. That was how it would look. Like she'd paid for it. She'd be much better off just paying someone to knock him off. Here in Chicago, she knew she could get that done for a hundred grand or less.

"Listen, Butch," she said with a huge sigh. "I can't just send you that much money at once. Not after what just happened today. Investigators are gonna be watching my every move for the next six months or so. But I am going to pay you every dollar of that damn money back. I'll be sending my driver to pick you up some time this evening. We'll have dinner and talk, figure out some kind of payment plan. Maybe I can invest ten or fifteen million into your construction company, make it all look legit, you know?"

"I'll be waiting," Butch said tersely and ended the call.

Johnna sat on her impossibly soft, white comforter for ten whole minutes, buzzing off the Percs she'd taken and the two shots of cognac she'd chased them down with. Finally, she raised her phone and texted her friend, Pandy, who was currently engaged to Luke the Producer, a big-time, Chicago, drill music producer and the CEO of Dark Side Records.

Pandy pushed open the bedroom door two minutes later. She was a 5'6" bombshell of a yellow bone with a body she'd paid good money to upgrade to its current curvaceous shape. Before Luke, she'd had a two-day fling with Drake, and before that, she'd dated Bam, a millionaire drug kingpin from the west side of Chicago. Pandy's shoulder-less Bottega dress was yellow in color and tight fitting. She had a croc-skin, Hermes Birkin bag hanging down from one shoulder and her iPhone 14 Plus clutched in one hand.

Johnna turned and looked at her without speaking. Her drug-clouded brain was working overtime, trying to decide whether or not she should ask the treacherous question that was sitting with its legs dangling over the front of her mind like SZA on her latest album cover.

"What's up, girl?" Pandy asked, taking a seat beside Johnna and draping an arm around her shoulders.

Johnna hesitated, eyeing the two missing nails on her left hand and licking at the stiches on the inside of her lower lip. Then, she drew in a heavy breath, exhaled, and blurted out the dreadful question.

"Do you know any hitmen? I need somebody killed, and I'll pay a hundred grand to get it done."

Chapter 18

As soon as Lacey walked through the door of Grizzy's 59th floor penthouse suite at the five-star Costilla Hotel in downtown Chicago, Nya ran to her, and the two women embraced and cried.

Grizzy and Marcus stood, watching the scene play out with their powerful arms folded across their barreled chests. They were cousins, but they could have easily passed as brothers. Marcus was an inch taller and maybe five pounds heavier than his older cousin, Grizzy. Both of them were dark in complexion with waves in their hair and the sort of zero-fat physiques that could only come from exerting oneself for hours on end in the gym.

Uptown and Smoke were seated around the table in the sitting room with Beto and Mozzy, the two GDs who'd come along with Marcus from the block he ran on 72nd and Green. The Dracos had stayed in their vehicles, but there were several handguns on the table — Glocks and Rugers and one Smith and Wesson, each one with an extended clip sticking out of the bottom. Scattered around the pistols were Styrofoam cups and crème soda bottles, three sacks of high-grade marijuana, five pint-sized bottles of Wockhardt promethazine with codeine, three fifths of Hennessy, and about seven or eight packs of Backwoods cigarillo blunt wraps.

The boys were rolling blunts, sipping iced Lean from their Styrofoam cups, and watching SportsCenter, but they all turned to stare at Lacey when she walked in. Three more young women came in behind her. Nya introduced them as Nu-Nu, Quita, and Brielle. The three girls were young, Black, and attractive, just like Nya and Lacey, and Grizzy chuckled at the swift change in his gang's disposition as the girls came over and made themselves comfortable on the sofas and chairs. The men went from griping about Lebron and the Lakers being crushed by the Nuggets in a 4-0 sweep to laughing and grinning as they introduced themselves to the girls. There were two pool tables in the suite, and before long, the drinks were flowing, the blunts were burning, and two pool games were underway.

Grizzy grabbed a pair of cue sticks and chalked the tips while Marcus racked the balls, both of them watching Nya and Lacey from the corners of their eyes as the two girls moved to one corner of the room to speak in private.

"So," Marcus asked, "what's the play? I thought we was s'posed to be slidin' through Keystone?"

"We is." Grizzy positioned the cue ball while Marcus removed the triangular rack from the table. "Just not now. They got news cameras out there right now. I just seen it on Fox32 before I left the crib. Police and news reporters. Gotta wait til later."

Marcus nodded his head thoughtfully. "They'll be gone in a couple hours," he said, cutting another glance at Lacey and Nya. He licked his lips in what seemed like slow motion. "G, I like that tall one. On fo'nem, she thick as hell. Look at all that ass, nigga. And she pretty as fuck. Damn, she remind me of Angel Reese, ol' girl that play for LSU."

Grizzy angled the stick between his first two fingers and slammed it forward into the cue ball. The colored balls scattered every which way. The nine-ball dropped in a side pocket, and when the balls came to a stop, Grizzy set his sights on the two-ball while he thought about Nya and the chance he'd had to blow her back out in his living room a few hours ago.

He had wanted to do it. Nya was, without a doubt, the most beautiful woman he'd ever had the opportunity to be intimate with. But at the time, he had just hung up from talking with his father, and his brain had been filled with numbers.

$30,000,000.

More money than he'd ever even *dreamed* of having.

"So, all we gotta do is snatch up some old school nigga?" Marcus asked, snatching Grizzy from his reverie.

Grizzy nodded. "Old school nigga named Butch. He had a few million dollars of my old man's money when the Feds did that sweep. I need all that."

"*We* need all that."

"You know I'ma break bread," Grizzy said, though he had his mind set on keeping the majority of the money for himself.

He won the game ten minutes later and absolutely refused to give Marcus a rematch, choosing instead to retire to the bedroom and leaving everyone else to party and socialize without him.

There was a lot for him to think about — Butch and the kidnapping scheme that hadn't yet pieced itself together in his head, the four fellow gang members he and Marcus had brought in on the plot and the reward they'd be expecting when all was said and done, Nya and the clear and present danger he'd unintentionally put her in.

He removed his shoes and stretched out in bed. He interlaced his fingers behind his head, crossed his ankles, and half listened to the rap song someone had turned on and cranked up to full volume in the sitting room. It was Lil Durk's *Hellcats and Trackhawks*, which made Grizzy think of his own Trackhawk, and Marcus's Charger Hellcat, and the Challenger Hellcat that had rolled right past them, pulled up in front of Nya's house, and showered it with bullets.

Grizzy shut his eyes and concentrated on his breathing. The few sips of liquor he'd drank before leaving home was practically gone from his bloodstream, but he was still feeling the effects of all the marijuana smoke he'd inhaled over the past couple of hours. It had him feeling drowsy and relaxed.

He was just starting to doze off when the click of the door opening startled him awake. He cracked open an eyelid, saw that Nya had just entered the room and was quietly pushing the door shut behind her, and quickly reclosed his eyes and tried to restrain the corners of his mouth from rising into a grin.

He failed miserably.

"I know you're up, old man," Nya said with a little snicker as she climbed into his bed beside him. "I saw you peeking. You ain't slick at all."

Grizzy opened his eyes and turned his head to look at her. He didn't say a word. He kept his mouth shut and studied Nya's sexy lips as she reached over to set her purse on the nightstand. She was the kind of girl who looked even prettier when she was intoxicated — her eyes red and asquint, a silly smile pasted on her gorgeous, round face.

"The police just called my phone and left a voicemail, asking me to either call and speak with them or come down to Area Five Headquarters for an interview," she said, turning onto her side to face Grizzy and resting her head on a fluffy, white pillow. "It's about my house being shot up and the trail of blood leading out the sidewalk. They called Lacey and left a message on her voicemail too. I told her to just ignore it for now. We'll come up with a story later."

"Definitely." Grizzy shifted his gaze to the television across from the front of the bed. TMZ Live was on. A photo of tech billionaire Johnna Broward showed briefly on the screen, then it switched to an aerial shot of the Panteon Tech building in Lower Manhattan, and finally, it went to a video clip that showed a fleet of black Escalades parked next to Johnna's private jet outside a private aircraft hangar at O'Hare International Airport.

"Did you know that Johnna Broward owns a condo a few blocks over from here?" Nya asked. "We can probably see it from that window." She put her hand on Grizzy's shirt and traced a random pattern with one long fingernail. "Can you imagine having two billion dollars? I wouldn't know what to do with that much money. I follow Johnna and her sisters on IG, and it seems like every day they're on another yacht, in another country, on another private jet. They just travel, travel, travel. Buy, buy, buy. Why can't I be rich like that?"

"You can. Just fuck with me. I'll get us there one day."

Nya's smile broadened, and she sat up and climbed on top of Grizzy. She stared down at him, sinking her teething into her lower lip, and for a while, they gazed into each other's bloodshot eyes. Then, she reached for the hem of his shirt and shoved it up to his chest, and for the next ten or fifteen seconds, she ran the soft palms of her hands back-and-forth over the chiseled rectangles of muscle that made up his six-pack. Two inches of pointed tongue came out from between her lips and curled upward. TMZ moved on to the next story — billionaire Amazon CEO Jeff Bezos and his girlfriend, Lauren Sanchez, were in Carnes, flaunting their engagement with a twenty-carat diamond ring and a massive superyacht that had cost Bezo $500 million — but that was mere background noise to Grizzy. Nya was sitting on the front of his designer jogging pants, but it felt like she had plopped down right on his lungs. He could hardly breathe. Her beauty was breathtaking.

"How many kids you got?" Nya asked, peeling her gaze from his chest to look him in the eyes.

"Just one. My daughter, Kamari. Why? You tryna have a baby or some'n?"

She shrugged. "One day maybe. I ain't in no rush. Now Lacey, on the other hand, she's another story. You better warn your cousin out there. She already talkin' about havin' his baby, and they just started talking five minutes ago."

Grizzy wasn't thinking about Lacey *or* Marcus. His hands were sliding forward along Nya's soft, reddish-brown thighs, and his dick was growing harder by the second.

"I'm telling you right now," Nya said, shifting her weigh around on his hardening length of muscle, "if you pull out your dick and put it right back in your pants again, I'm fuckin' you up. You gon' have to fight me in this bitch."

Chuckling, Grizzy said, "You know, I rented this suite specifically for you. I thought of that story you told me about ol' boy who brought you to a suite and fed you strawberries and did all that other romantic shit. That's what I had in mind when I picked this penthouse suite."

"Kinda hard to be romantic when you got five more niggas and four bitches in the other room." Nya's eyes were glued to his chest, her hands caressing his brick-hard pectoral muscles. "But you know what?" she asked, lowering her already soft voice a few octaves. "I don't really like all that romantic shit anyway. I like a grimy, gangsta-ass nigga, and that shit you did earlier turned me on more than a strawberry ever could. You didn't show no fear." She leaned forward and kissed him on the lips. "Just jumped out and blicked them niggas."

She kissed him again, but this time, the kiss went on and on and on, her head turning from one side to the other, until Grizzy's hands were rubbing and squeezing her ass on their own accord, and his dick was straining against his black cotton Amiri joggers. Grizzy had never thought much of kissing — in fact, due to his belief that most women had sucked at least one dick some time recently, he usually shunned kissing altogether — but sucking and smooching Nya's pretty lips seemed like the right thing to do, so he just went with it.

Seconds later, Nya lifted her head, rose up on her knees, and moved backward, her glassy-eyed gaze shifting to the erotic mountain at the front of his joggers. She curled her fingers around his waistband and pulled down both his joggers and his boxer-briefs in one hurried motion. His dick flopped out and landed with an audible smack on his stomach.

Nya moved down and ran the flat of her tongue along the underside of his length. She looked up at him as she did it, and Grizzy thought that was the sexiest shit ever.

He picked up his erection and slapped its head on the flat of her tongue. Then, she took his dick in both hands and started stroking it, smacking it off her cheek. "It's been a minute since I put my mouth on a man," she said. "You better appreciate this shit."

Yeah, right, Grizzy thought, though a part of him believed it was true.

He closed his eyes and interlaced his fingers behind his head as her tight, wet mouth started going up and down on him, slowly and steadily. Every few seconds, she'd pop it out of her mouth to lick and suck on the head, and then, she'd go down again, stroking him in both hands as she did it.

Nya's fellatio skills were beyond exceptional. She really started to get into it after a couple of minutes, pausing to spit on the tip before stroking the saliva up and down his length and sucking it back into her mouth. She shoved it to the back of her throat and gagged herself for several seconds. She took his balls in her mouth and sucked on them while jerking his dick in one hand, and then, she went back to fellating him, her soft, pink lips gliding up and down his long, hard muscle. The actual length of his erection was 9 ¾ inches; he had measured it three or four times in the past.

He looked down and saw that Nya had tied her waterfall of silky, black hair into a ponytail. She was such a little woman, and her head game packed a serious punch. He felt like he could spend the rest of his life with his dick sliding in and out of her mouth.

When he felt the familiar tingle in his scrotum that signaled an imminent eruption, he cupped her chin in one hand and lifted her tightly sucking mouth off of him. "Damn, shorty. Hold on a second," he said, breathing heavily.

Nya showed a silly grin and giggled innocently. She wiped the ring of saliva from around her mouth with the back of her hand, stared at his spit-coated erection for a couple of seconds, and pulled his joggers and boxer-briefs all the way down his legs and off his feet. Then, she stood up on the bed, undid her shorts, and stepped out of them. She wasn't wearing any panties. Her pussy was hairless, her labia pretty and plump, and the area between those meaty pink vaginal lips was glistening with moisture.

She turned her back to him and, with her feet planted on either side of him, walked backward until she was standing over his face and dropped down onto her knees so that her pussy was right above his mouth and his dick was right below hers.

Grizzy didn't hesitate. He lifted his head just enough for his nose to touch her pussy and stuck out his tongue, inhaling the delicious scent of her sex as he dug in for a taste. Her pussy did not disappoint. It tasted just as good as it smelled. Grizzy placed his large, veiny, black hands on her butt cheeks and spread them apart as he began sucking on her pussy, doing his best to get her clitoris in his mouth too.

Nya's juices were copious, practically gushing onto his probing tongue as he licked and sucked. She turned her head, rested the side of her face on the underside of his hard dick, and moaned with her brow furrowed and her mouth wide open.

Grizzy had a few decades of experience when it came to the art of cunnilingus. Joya Kelly, his daughter's mother, had always loved it when he ate her pussy. It had been the one sure way to put a smile on her face and keep it there for at least seven or eight hours, and he could tell by Nya's reaction to the feel of his swiftly flickering tongue that she was loving it too.

He hadn't been at it long when Nya suddenly yelped and slammed down onto his mouth. "Oh, shit. Oh, shit. Oh, shit," she screeched, and then, she began to shake, as if experiencing a seizure, and a wave of creamy juices poured out onto his tongue and chin.

Grizzy blew on her quivering pussy while she shivered her way through the orgasm. He delivered a sharp smack to her right ass cheek and reached over to the nightstand for her purse. He found the box of Magnums, took one out, and used his teeth to tear open the wrapper.

"That's the best fuckin' head I ever had in my life," Nya said, lying flat on his chest and abs with her pussy juices still dripping down onto his neck.

No longer tired, Grizzy put on the condom and got out of bed, picking Nya up in his arms as his socked feet hit the floor. He crossed the room to the huge floor-to-ceiling windows and yanked down on the beaded cord that sent the fresh gray curtains flying open.

Nya turned her head to look out the window. So did Grizzy. Together, they took in the breathtaking view of downtown Chicago and the great lake beyond. It wasn't yet five o'clock p.m. The sun was still a searing hot ball of orange in a nearly cloudless sky.

Turning his attention back to Nya, Grizzy guided his condom-sheathed dick into her slippery opening and watched her mouth fall open again as he positioned his arms under her legs and pressed her back against the windowpane.

"Ooouuu," she moaned. "Take off your shirt. I wanna see your chest."

Grizzy maneuvered out of his black Amiri shirt and threw it toward the bed, and then, he was sliding in and out of Nya's snugly gripping pussy while she dug her fingernails into his shoulders and stared at him with her mouth and eyes agape.

Her pussy was incredibly wet, and the saliva he'd left down there had very little to do with it. Wet, squishy sounds came out of her every time he slid in and every time he slid out. And her tight vaginal walls squeezed him better than his own fist ever could.

"Damn," he said after just five minutes of thrusting in and out of her. "I don't wanna nut, but I feel it comin'."

"Ooouuu, shit" was Nya's breathless reply. Grizzy was holding her by the waist, going in deeper and deeper with every forward thrust. She tried sliding up the windowpane to get away from him, but he tightened his grip on her waist and slammed her down onto his long, hard muscle.

"Ohhhh, shhiiiit," she half-shouted. "I'm cumming again! I'm cumming a…"

Her fingernails sank deeper into his flesh, and she came when he came like in the movies. Grizzy felt her inner muscles contracting around his erection as his dick spasmed and spilled an ounce of thick white semen into the tip of his condom.

STEPPERS | KING RIO

Chapter 19

With more than twelve thousand of the Windy City's most powerful and wealthiest citizens under its continued surveillance, "CPD Black" was the Chicago Police Department's answer to the NYPD's Red Unit, and Lieutenant Brad Voight ran the clandestine police unit like an elite Federal agency.

Voight, a thirty-year CPD veteran, had established the Black Unit in early 2020 with $150 million in taxpayer dollars and another $1.4 billion in donations from wealthy individuals who, at the time, were concerned that the Black Lives Matter protests would spill over into their neck of the woods. CPD Black's headquarters — a 17,000 square-foot warehouse in Chicago's predominately white Wrigleyville neighborhood — had cost a cool $8.6 million, and an additional $51.9 million had gone into converting the enormous warehouse into one of the most technologically advanced office building in the city.

To avoid publicity, CPD Black operated under the guise of Secure Force, a private security firm that catered exclusively to the city's elite. Quite often, the Black Unit found itself working alongside the FBI to take down criminal organizations they felt had grown strong enough to extort the insanely rich, but every now and then, the insanely rich found themselves in the crosshairs of CPD Black.

As was the case with Panteon CEO Johnna Broward.

Broward's questionable decision to hire the dangerous felon, who'd slain four of her employees, and her even more questionable decision to flee New York immediately afterward, had drawn scrutiny not only from the FBI but also from NYPD Red's Detective Rick McKenzie, who'd made a call to Lt. Voight shortly after Broward's Gulfstream jet took off from JFK.

By the time the private jet landed at O'Hare, Secure Force had intercepted Broward's request for armed security and sent a ten-man team of undercover CPD Black officers to meet her on the tarmac in a fleet of B5-armored luxury SUVs.

And it hadn't taken them long to catch Johnna Broward in a compromising position.

At exactly five o'clock in the afternoon, Voight stood, leaning forward with his hands gripping the railing of the suspended steel walkway that overlooked the first-floor office spaces. There were rows and rows of long, gray tables with large, high-tech computer monitors in front of them. The men and women seated at the tables wore earpieces and standard office attire. The majority of the computer monitors showed live camera feeds from wealthy neighborhoods across the city.

Voight turned on his heel and headed into his office. He had just phoned Detective McKenzie in New York, and the AirPod Pros were ringing in his ears.

McKenzie answered. "Tell me what you got, Voight."

Voight laughed his bottomless, guttural laugh. He was fifty-four years old, but he looked thirty, and he was in damn good shape. Six feet even. A hundred and ninety pounds. Handsome in a rich, white guy kind of way.

"Broward's fucking the help," he said, walking to the dartboard on his office wall and plucking the eight darts from the target. "Jayvon Sullivan, the guy who…"

"Killed Michael Caldwell," McKenzie finished.

"Exactly. They did the wild thing in the back of one of our SUVs. She raised the privacy partition, and they got right to it."

After a moment of silence, McKenzie said, "I didn't see that coming, but there's not much we can do about her fucking the security guy. He gave a statement on the shooting and turned over his weapon, and everything he alleged is backed up by the camera footage. He's clean as far as we're concerned."

"There's more," Voight said, throwing a dart. It hit the bull's eye with a solid thump. "Broward's sending one of my men to pick up some guy named Devonte' Gibbs for dinner at eight. He goes by Butch. And get this — Butch and Caldwell were close friends back in the day. They were even arrested together once for shooting up a car full of Mickey Cobras the Black P. Stones were at war with back in '98."

"Wow, that's something."

"Yeah. We're working with FBI Special Agent Jacob Walloby on this, and his IT guy just hacked into Butch's emails not even twenty minutes ago. Turns out it was Butch who talked Broward into hiring Caldwell from the start. He sent her fourteen emails about it the week Caldwell was released from prison. It's clear from these emails that she knew Caldwell was a violent felon and former member of the Black P. Stones from Altgeld Gardens, where Johnna Broward herself was born and raised. A guy named Willie White was the leader of that particular faction of Black Stones, and Butch and Caldwell were key members of his inner circle. But that's nothing. There's another piece to this puzzle that *really* got me to scratching my head."

"Yeah? What's that?"

"*Johnny* Broward. Bang Boy. The shooter Willie White used to knock off all his enemies. He's Johnna Broward's older brother, and he's actually cellmates with Willie White at that federal prison in Terre Haute, Indiana."

Another stony silence from McKenzie. Voight threw another dart, his cocky grin on full display. He could practically feel the cogs turning in McKenzie's head.

"It's all starting to make sense now, ain't it?" Voight said.

"I just thought of something," said McKenzie. "I'll call you back."

The call ended, and Voight's triumphant grin never left his face as he threw the rest of his darts. He'd never taken down a billionaire before, but there was a first time for everything.

Chapter 20

After Grizzy fell asleep, Nya sat up next to him in bed, scrolling through Facebook on her smartphone, with a content smile on her angelic face.

She was barely even looking at her phone. Her brain kept replaying the sexual bliss she'd experienced at the hands of Lejon "Grizzy" White.

He had fucked her again after his first orgasm. In fact, he'd lifted her right off his dick and placed her legs on his shoulders after that first nut, and he'd sucked and licked on her clitoris until she grabbed hold of his ears and trembled through a third seismic orgasm. By then, his dick was hard again, and he'd carried her to the bed, put on another condom, and fucked her doggystyle for a good twenty minutes — holding her hips in a firm grip, rubbing his hands along her ass and lower back, occasionally pulling out to smack his considerable length across her ass before ramming it back inside of her.

That had been over an hour ago. They had showered together in the adjoining bathroom and donned the hotel's plush white robes before returning to bed. She'd dozed off on his chest and awakened a little over a half an hour ago. The time at the top of her phone screen read 6:38 p.m. She'd been on Facebook for twenty minutes now, and in that time, she'd learned a lot.

The boys who shot up her house were Cold Gang members. Their names were Tavaris and Montez. Both were hospitalized with multiple gunshot wounds they'd suffered during their brief standoff with police, but Nya didn't care about any of that. The only thing she took from the knowledge of their identities was that she could not return home under any circumstances. At least not anytime soon. Every single member of the Cold Gang knew where she lived — several of them had lain in Lacey's bed at one time or another — and with both Cold Gang and Wicked Town being upset with her, she knew that going back home would mean a death sentence.

Regardless of the danger she'd put herself in, Nya didn't regret helping Grizzy at all. She knew a good man when she saw one, and Grizzy fit the description to the letter. And besides, there was clearly a silver lining in all that had happened. She'd gained a new man, a man who was a lot more handsome and physically attractive than any man she'd had in the past, and even if things didn't work out between the two of them, she still had $5,100 in her purse to show for it, and Lacey had $5,000 in hers. That was more than enough money for them to find a new place.

As if reading Nya's mind, the bedroom door was pushed open at that very second, and Lacey stuck her head in for a peek around.

"Mmmm, girrrl," Lacey said, beaming. "You put that nigga to *sleep*, didn't you?"

Nya flipped her a middle finger and slipped out of bed to go to the door. "Bitch, what the fuck do you want?" she asked, stepping out of the bedroom and pulling the door shut behind her, not only to give Grizzy his privacy but also to keep her from waking him.

And there was a lot of noise. A Rooga song was playing at full volume. Nu-Nu and Brielle were sitting on one of the pool tables, laughing and talking loudly, drinking cognac from blue plastic cups, and recording videos on their smartphones, while Marcus, Mozzy, and Uptown shot dice on the other pool table. Quita had stripped down to her bra and panties and climbed into the jacuzzi with Smoke.

Beto was fast asleep on the sofa with a sliver of drool dangling precariously from the corner of his thick-lipped mouth.

Nya stayed close to the bedroom door; she was barefoot, plus she didn't trust leaving Grizzy in such a vulnerable position while so many other men were in the suite with them. They were his so-called fellow gang members, but gang members turned on each other all the time. That was why Nya believed it was a woman's job to be her man's first line of defense.

"Tavaris shot up our house," Lacey said, placing her hand on the soft shoulder of Nya's bathrobe to keep her balance. She'd obviously had too much to drink. "Ol' bitch ass nigga was just in my inbox last week, and he gon' go and shoot up our house. I'm glad twelve shot his lil, ugly ass."

"I'm so sorry for getting us into this. You told me to mind my business, and I didn't listen." Unconsciously, Nya scissored her legs and rose up on her toes. Grizzy had beaten her poor little vagina into submission, leaving a slight ache in her swollen vaginal lips.

Lacey noticed the move and squinted at her. "Why you movin' like that?"

"Like what?" Nya asked with a telling smirk.

"Hoe, you know what the fuck I'm talkin' about. Why you all on yo' tippy toes? That nigga done blew yo' back out like that?"

Smirking, Nya rolled her eyes. "Did you see what happened to Johnna Broward? She got beat up by the man who shot all them people at the Panteon building in New York. They got footage of her at O'Hare a couple hours after the shooting."

"She's a smart bitch. I would've left New York too. My whole "Empire State of Mind" would've been gone the second I heard them gunshots. But look, we need to get somebody over there to fix our front door. I'm about to text old man Butch and see if I can get him to go and do it. We'll just wait a couple of days and then hire some movers to pack up our stuff and put it in storage 'cause you know we can't go back home. That shit over with. Crunchy's soft ass snitched on you."

Nya barely heard that last part. Her mind was stuck on what Lacey had just said about Butch.

"Go ahead and text him," she said and pushed open the bedroom door. "I gotta wake Renzo up."

Chapter 21

Demetria "Dee-Dee" Earl was known around Chicago as the "Queen of Catering," and she was clearly in charge of things when she and her team of acclaimed chefs arrived at Johnna's condo with three-rolling carts of main courses, side dishes, drinks, and desserts.

The opioids Johnna had taken a few hours earlier had her feeling a bit woozy, but the drugs had made the stinging pain in her bottom lip nonexistent, and that was how she preferred it to be. She sat right at the middle of her obnoxiously long, thirty seat, redwood, dining table with her twenty-two-year-old sister, Jonesha, to her left and their mother, April, to her right. As Dee-Dee and her assistants filled their plates with savory slabs of lamb, crab cakes, lobster, four-cheese macaroni, mashed potatoes with white gravy, and mouthwatering buttermilk biscuits, Johnna kept glancing across the table at Pandy.

Johnna wasn't really feeling Pandy's idea, which was to wait a couple of weeks for things to die down before ordering the hit on Butch. Pandy said she knew the perfect person for the job — some gang banger named Jab from the North Lawndale neighborhood on Chicago's west side —but now wasn't the time to be getting anyone killed. It would be better to just string Butch along for the next couple of weeks, send him and his family on a nice paid vacation to some exotic Caribbean Island with all the bells and whistles. That should leave Butch with his guards down, and Pandy would have Jab lying in wait for him when he returned home.

The main problem Johnna had with Pandy's plan wasn't the cost. Pandy had suggested a budget of $500,000 to get the job done with $250,000 of it going to Jab for the hit and the rest going toward the cost of Butch's vacation and Pandy's $150,000 fee for arranging it all, and Johnna figured that was much better than paying Butch the $22 million she still owed him. No, Johnna's main issue with Pandy's plan was that Butch would have several more weeks to live while her longtime assistant, Black Ant, didn't have another second to live.

Johnna had loved Black Ant with all her heart. He'd scheduled her every waking hour, from her visits to the gym four mornings a week to her boardroom meetings and weekly flights to Chicago to visit her family. He'd been her shopping partner, her best friend, her confidant. Johnna had introduced him to his husband, Edrell Scott, during a yacht party in Ibiza two years ago, and she'd attended their Baltimore wedding late last September and allowed them to use her two-hundred-foot mega yacht for their honeymoon cruise to Montego Bay, Jamaica.

The Browards had a long-standing rule about cell phones at the dinner table. Johnna broke that sacred rule when she picked up her iPhone to wire Pandy the $500,000, and no one said a word. Next, she got up and stepped away to make a quick FaceTime call to Butch, being sure to put in her AirPods and walk all the way out of the room to keep her family and friends from overhearing the conversation.

Butch was sitting down this time, in a room with lavender colored walls and bright rays of sunlight spilling from somewhere offscreen. A hue of cigarette smoke swayed up into the air next to his face. A dog barked, and he glanced down near his feet before looking back up at Johnna.

"Good afternoon, Butch," Johnna said in her kindest tone of voice.

Butch only looked at her. He brought his Newport 100 up to his mouth for a drag and didn't say a word. The dog barked twice more.

"I'm gonna have to cancel that dinner date," Johnna said, "but I've got something even better. I uhh… I'd like to send you and your family on a nice vacation for the next couple of weeks. All expenses paid. You pick the island, the hotel rooms, the activities, and I'll handle the bill. I'll even give you fifty grand in spending money, so you'll never have to spend a dollar out of your own pocket, and when you get back, we'll meet for lunch and figure out the smartest way for me to wire you that $22 million without raising any eyebrows. How does that sound?"

Butch streamed smoke out of his nostrils for a moment. His expression remained hard and unyielding. Then, it relaxed a little, and he said, "Why can't we meet for dinner at eight o'clock like we planned?"

"Because I'm in *pain*, Butch. I was assaulted this morning, and four of my best employees were gunned down while I watched from my office computer. And *also* because two NYPD detectives came to the hospital room I was in with questions about Caldwell. I can't meet up with anyone right now. That's why I want you to go on this trip with your family and enjoy yourself while all this blows over. By the time you get back, I'll be ready to wire you at least the first $10 million."

Butch hesitated. He ran the hand holding his cigarette over the top of his bald head, scrunched his face, as if he was about to sneeze, and rubbed his nose with the palm of his hand. Johnna thought it might be a side effect of his years of drug abuse.

"Rio de Janeiro," he said after a time. "That's where I wanna go with my family. I want an all-expense paid vacation to Rio de Janeiro, Brazil. And I want to stay in a mansion, not a hotel. I want two Bentleys for us to ride around in while we're there and a yacht we can get on to sail the ocean whenever we get the urge."

"Done. I'll have my new assistant text you within the next hour or so. Go ahead and start packing because I'll be sending you all out on a private jet first thing tomorrow."

Butch narrowed his eyes on her. He seemed to weigh her words, trying to decide whether he could trust her or not. "I'll be waitin'," he said and hung up.

Johnna let out a weighty sigh and turned to look into the dining room. Her family was looking at her, waiting on her, so they could join hands, say grace, and eat.

"Hope you enjoy yourself in Brazil, old Butch," she mouthed silently as she walked back toward her seat at the table. "It'll be the last trip you ever take."

Chapter 22

'Not sure if ur busy but I really need u 2 send somebody 2 fix my door. Somebody shot up my house and kicked in the door. Guess they thought it was somebody else's house. But I can't lock my door now & I really need u. I'll do u a big favor if you can get over here asap.'

'OK. Give me 30 minutes. Sending one of my boys to grab a door now. I'll let you know the cost when I get there. We can work out the payment later.'

Nya handed her phone to Grizzy, so he could see the screenshot Lacey had just sent her. It showed the message thread between Lacey and Butch.

"See?" Nya said. "I told you we got this. Let us finesse this old nigga. We'll flirt with him a little, he'll tell us everything, and you won't have to kidnap him or torture him or none of that other crazy shit you had in your fucked up head."

Grizzy laughed and shook his head then turned his attention to the message on her phone screen and started reading it.

They were sitting in his Trackhawk, parked in the alleyway behind her house on Central Avenue. His cousin's slime green Dodge Charger Hellcat was parked right behind them. Beto was the only one out of the car; he was bent over, clutching his knees and vomiting into a hedge of bushes bordering a neighbor's chain link fence. Lacey was in the

Charger with Marcus and Mozzy. The other girls had opted to stay at the hotel and wait for everyone else to return.

Nya was a tad bit nervous, but she felt safe with Grizzy looking after her. He had his Draco on his lap, and every couple of seconds, he'd check the rearview and sideview mirrors and also the Jeep's 360° cameras to make sure nobody was creeping up on them. Uptown and Smoke were posted up in the backseat with their own mini assault rifles loaded and ready. If anyone came through the alleyway on some bullshit, they wouldn't have very long to be on it.

"Have Marcus pull around front and park one or two houses down," Nya said, strategizing. "That way if somebody pulls up, trying to shoot at my house while I'm in there, Mozzy and Marcus can air em out before I end up with a bullet in my ass."

Grizzy nodded. "I got you." He picked up his own phone and typed out a text message to Marcus. Seconds later, the Charger's powerful Hellcat engine roared to life. Lacey's door swung open, and she climbed out with one hand stuck down in her purse. Nya did the same thing, and together, she and Lacey hurried into their backyard, up the concrete walkway, and onto their back porch.

There were several holes in the wall next to the door. The holes were roughly the size and shape of a quarter, and Nya spotted another one high up on the door as she slipped her key into the keyhole and turned it.

She took the Glock pistol from inside her purse, and Lacey pulled a Glock from inside hers. Cautiously pushing open the door, Nya stepped into the house with her gun raised. They went from the kitchen, to the living room, to the bedrooms and bathroom, and then, they checked the basement to make sure no one was down there before heading back upstairs to survey the damage the high-caliber rifle rounds had done to their place.

The bullet holes were everywhere. In the living room, their sectional sofa had taken five rounds to the back. The television had one large hole in the bottom left-hand corner and another right through the center. The wall was packed with holes, the floor below them littered with drywall. In the kitchen, Nya discovered a hole in the side of her beloved stainless steel Kenmore refrigerator, and when she opened it, she saw that the bullet had slammed through a pitcher of lemon-lime Kool-Aid and a carton of Tropicana orange juice. The roll of Bounty paper towels she used to mop up the juice had suffered a graze wound from the gunfire, and when she checked her bedroom, she saw that one round had torn through the lamp shade on her nightstand.

Wasting no time, Nya went straight to her closet, grabbed the large, red suitcase she'd purchased for the girls' trip to Miami she and Lacey had taken with a few of their friends two summers ago, and started filling it with clothes from her dresser drawers.

"We need to start packing right now," she yelled to Lacey. "That way, we can put our thing down on Butch as soon as he get there and be ready to leave at the same time."

"Already on it," Lacey shouted back.

Nya put in an AirPod and phoned Grizzy as she stripped herself of the clothes she'd worn all day and slipped into a pair of blue and white Ethika leggings and a matching top. Grizzy didn't answer the call, so she googled his government name to see what came up and found his Instagram page just as a text from him popped up in her notifications.

'Otp w my daughter.'

"Hm." Nya started to roll her eyes, caught herself doing it, and smiled at her selfish response. "It's his *daughter*, Nya," she muttered aloud to herself. "Can't be jelly of the daughter. You'll run him off before you even get him."

"Bitch, why are you in here talkin' to yourself?" It was Lacey. She had appeared in the doorway behind Nya.

"No reason." Nya turned to face Lacey but kept her eyes on her phone screen. She was drooling over a video Grizzy had posted of himself doing pull-ups in the gym, but somehow, she managed to stay focused on what was important. "You heard back from Butch?"

Lacey nodded. "He down there on Laramie and Chicago Avenue, getting gas. Said he'll be down here in a second." She crossed her arms and leaned against the door frame. Nya could see that the knuckles on her left hand were a little swollen from punching Crunchy's lights out. "Explain to me what the hell it is we're doing with Butch anyway. Why do we need to get him to tell us about some money?"

"Because it's thirty million dollars' worth of money," Nya said brightly.

"Wait, *what*? Thirty *million*? You serious?"

"Mm hmm. Don't just come out and say it though. We gotta play the sexy role. I would say we can kiss and all that to get him all warmed up, but ain't no tellin' where yo' mouth been."

"I don't be puttin' my mouth on nobody." Lacey stuck out her tongue and smiled around it. "And besides, I might be off the market anyway. Marcus talkin' 'bout he single and need a bad bitch like me by his side. And you know he's my type. He's tall, dark, handsome, and you can look at him and tell he got money. Maybe not thirty million dollars' worth of money," she added with a laugh, "but he definitely got money."

Nya smirked and nodded and started looking at the comments under Grizzy's video. There was one from a Joya Kelly that read, 'Okay, I see you, baby daddy!!' Nya touched the woman's name and scrolled through a couple of Joya's photos. She was a gorgeous, brown-skinned woman with captivating, light brown eyes, rich, dark hair, that was almost as long and silky as Nya's, thick thighs, and a fat, round ass that instantly made Nya feel insecure. There were photos of Joya with an older man in doctor's scrubs and even more photos of her with a bad ass, dark-skinned girl who was clearly Grizzy's daughter. Joya looked like a happily married woman, but Nya already didn't like her.

"What the fuck are you doin'?" Lacey asked as she walked over to look at Nya's phone. She'd hardly even gotten a glimpse when her own phone rang with a call from Butch just as Nya's rang with a call back from Grizzy. They both answered the calls. Lacey said, "He's here," and left the bedroom to greet Butch at the door.

"You heard that?" Nya said to Grizzy. "He just pulled up. Stay on the line and listen to us finesse this old creep outta thirty Ms."

Chapter 23

Butch parked his F250 at the curb in front of Lacey and her friend, Nya's house, and adjusted the rearview mirror to study his appearance in its reflection. He was smiling harder than ever, dressed in a simple bright tee and cargo shorts. While his family was at home packing for their spur-of-the-moment, South American vacation, he was sliding through on a bad young bitch to get his dick sucked one last time before he left. He'd be a different man when he returned, a man with at least $10 million in legitimate Panteon Tech dollars in his bank account. He'd leave his construction company to his son and retire to his ranch in Amarillo, Texas. Buy himself a couple of horses and maybe some cattle. A boat. Sports bar. He had close to a million dollars in the bank now, and Johnna was right, he'd have a helluva lot more had he not blown through millions of dollars on his many addictions — namely sex with younger women, crack cocaine, powder cocaine, alcohol, and gambling — but he'd recovered, and now, he was ready to live.

Jarrell, one of Butch's employees, pulled in behind him in a new-model GMC Sierra. Lacey's new door was in the back of Jarrell's pickup along with the tools they'd need to install it. Butch would pay Jarrell for the work, but he wasn't planning on accepting any money from Lacey. He wanted something else from her.

"I'm outside," he said, holding his phone up in front of his mouth as he climbed out of his pickup, one of his numerous pockets bulging with cash. He'd left the house with a few grand in his pocket — three thousand dollars to be exact — and he planned to use it to convince Lacey to agree to the proposition he had in mind.

"Okay," she said. "I'm coming to the door now."

As Butch and Jarrell carried the new door up the steps to Lacey's front porch, Butch narrowed his eyes at the trail of blood droplets, and Jarrell said, "Did somebody get shot over here or some'n?"

They leaned against the porch railing and furrowed their brows at the bullet holes in the kicked-in door, and in the large picture window, and all over the front of the house.

"What the hell happened over here?" Butch asked Lacey as she lifted the front door on its damaged hinges to pull it open. "Is this the house they say got shot up before the police shot those two young boys from over my way?"

Lacey nodded her head. She had on a simple black tee with Rihanna on the front and tight black sweatpants, but she still looked like the kind of girl Butch had lusted over during his time in prison, the really thick girls from urban booty magazines like *Straight Stuntin*, *Go Viral*, and *Kite DM*. Her friend, Nya, was standing behind her, looking like a snack in that tight little outfit of hers. She wasn't thick like Lacey, but she was as bad and sexy as they come.

Butch stepped inside, looked around at the bullet-riddled living room area, and closed his arms around Lacey's waist for a hug. "Mind if I talk to you in the back for a minute?"

"No, that's fine. But you know Nya's my girlfriend now, right? Like, we're in a sexual relationship, but we still kinda date men here and there."

Butch's eyes lit up. He looked from Lacey to Nya and back to Lacey with an incredulous expression on his face. Were they kidding? They *had* to be kidding. There was no way in hell he was going to get this lucky. Or was there?

"Okay, that's cool," he said. "She can come too. Shit, I'm sure she'll wanna get in on this. It's the kinda offer you won't be able to refuse."

Jarrell said he was going back to his pickup to get his toolbox and start on the door, and Butch let Lacey and Nya lead him down a short hallway and into a neatly arranged bedroom.

There was damage from the shooting in here as well. Butch spotted a hole in a lamp shade and mattress stuffing sprouting from a hole in the comforter on the queen-size bed. A suitcase full of women's clothing lay open at the foot of the bed, and a pistol with an extended magazine was sticking up out of a blue, leather purse next to the suitcase.

"I'll get somebody over here to spackle all these bullet holes," Butch said. He leaned back against the dresser, dug in one of his cargo shorts pockets, and pulled out $3,000 in cash — a hundred crisp new twenty-dollar bills and ten crisp new blue-faced hundreds. He spread it out in his hands. "Not that you'll need to stay in this house anymore. If y'all accept my offer, I'll have y'all livin' like Johnna Broward, put up in a penthouse downtown somewhere. That's my word. On Chief Malik."

As if on cue, both of the girls planted their hands on their hips, and Nya said, "What's the goddamn offer?"

"For real," Lacey added, "'cause right now, you doin' a whole lotta talkin' and ain't sayin' shit. How you gon' have us livin' like Johnna Broward?"

The cunning smile that spread across Butch's mouth spanned the entire width of his narrow, brown face. "Speakin' of Johnna Broward, she the one who'll be financin' this whole — you know what? Never mind all that. Just know this. I'm about to jump on a private jet first thing tomorrow morning and fly off to Brazil with my wife and kids for a couple of weeks, and when I get back, I'll have $10 million sittin' in my bank account. Now, I know y'all know I'm a married man, but y'all also know I like a lil some'n-some'n on the side every now and then. If y'all can agree to be that some'n, I'll give y'all this three Gs right now and another ninety-seven thousand as soon as I get back from Brazil."

The girls turned to look at each other, then Lacey turned back to Butch and said, "So, Johnna Broward's involved in all this? Tell us more about that."

Looking down at the cash in his hand, Butch took a few seconds to ponder whether or not it was wise to reveal the truth about his situation with Johnna Broward. It wouldn't be his first time telling someone that Johnna had stolen $23 million from him and used it to start the company. He'd told the story a hundred times to a hundred different people, and the only person who'd believed him was his wife.

"Y'all might not believe this," he said, raising his eyes from his handful of cash, "but when I got out the Feds six years ago, I came home to a little over thirty-million dollars in drug money. I had been holding it for a friend of mine when we all got indicted, and since he ended up with a life sentence, I kept the money for myself."

"So, how did Johnna Broward get involved with it?" Lacey asked.

"She stole $23 million from me and used it to get Panteon off the ground. Her brother, Bang Boy, was like," he twisted his index and middle fingers together, "with Willie White. He knew all about the money, and when Johnna came to him sayin' she was havin' a hard time findin' investors, he sent her at me."

"And you let her *steal* twenty-three *million* dollars from you?" Nya asked, moving her hands from her hips and folding her arms across her chest. "How in the world was she able to steal that much money at once? And what happened to the other $7 million?"

"It's a long story." Butch took his pack of cigarettes from his pocket and pulled one from the pack. "To make it short, she got me drunk as a skunk and high as a kite, and soon as

I passed out, she robbed me. My dumbass was tryna impress the bitch. Fucked up and showed her where I stashed the money. That other seven million got blown on dumb shit. I ain't even gon' lie to you. Drugs, casinos, and young, pretty bitches like you and Lacey. Had a lotta fun down there in Vegas. By the time I cleaned up and went to rehab, I was down to three hundred and eighty grand. Used that to buy some more property and start my construction company."

He lit a cigarette and filled his lungs with smoke, and as he did it, he realized that Nya and Lacey were listening to him as if they really believed him. They were hanging on to his every word.

"Okay, I'm in," Lacey said, taking the money from his hand. "And we gon' need that other ninety-seven thousand as soon as you get back from Brazil."

Nya's hand made a dramatic return to her hips. "Well, I'm not in. Lacey is my bitch and all, but I ain't fuckin' no old man."

Chapter 24

NYPD Red's Detective Rick McKenzie kept glancing at his gold Rolex wristwatch. The time was 9:05 p.m. Eastern, and he'd been sitting at the small, square table in his kitchen for almost three hours now, going over the Panteon Tech security camera footage on his laptop computer. He kept rewinding the footage from inside Johnna Broward's office, watching as Michael Caldwell rammed his shoulder into the door until it broke away from the frame, watching as Johnna hid beneath her desk until Caldwell reached under it, picked her up by the neck, and screamed something in her face, watching as she grabbed his wrist in both hands and frantically scissored her airborne legs until he backhanded her and sent her across the room.

Watching. Watching. Watching.

He watched Jayvon Sullivan shoot Caldwell dead, then switched to the hallway camera outside of Johnna's office and watched as Johnna and eight of her employees fled to the stairwell at the end of the hall, then switched to the stairwell cameras and watched as Johnna hurried down several flights of stairs among a rush of other panic-stricken Panteon employees, then switched to the first-floor cameras and watched as Johnna and dozens of other Panteon workers sprinted across the lobby and out the front doors.

Three empty cups of spicy, chicken flavored noodles stood next to McKenzie's computer, along with his Juul vape pen, his badge, and his holstered Glock Model 23 pistol. He sat back in his chair, picked up his vape pen, sucked on it, and blew a dense stream of smoke at the rapidly spinning ceiling fan above him.

"How'd you break those pretty, little fingernails, Johnna?" McKenzie muttered, shutting his eyes and breathing in deep. "How'd you do it?"

Panteon's cameras were among the most high-tech camera systems available in the security industry, the definition so crystal-clear that McKenzie could see the tiny specks of dust on Johnna's computer screen — and the two missing fingernails on her left hand, which McKenzie had just noticed were already gone before Michael Caldwell broke into her office.

He sat forward and brought up the camera inside Johnna's office. He rewound it until she left out to visit the restroom seventeen minutes before the shooting commenced, but there was nothing there. The fingernails were already broken when she entered the hallway restroom.

"You're a billionaire, Johnna," McKenzie mouthed silently. "No billionaire walks into the office with broken fingernails."

He kept going, retracing Johnna's movements as she left her office again, this time with her assistant, Anthony Ferguson, in tow. She walked through the building, sticking her head into offices, stopping to speak with this person and that person, visiting the cafeteria for what looked like some sort of breakfast burrito. Normal activities for a hands-on business owner.

McKenzie was just starting to lose confidence in his idea to rewind the footage when he finally found what he was looking for. He stopped the footage just before the incident began and watched it at regular speed.

Johnna and her assistant were on the second floor, walking past two middle aged, Black women, who had just exited one of the elevators. One of the women — the shorter, heavier one — said something to Johnna that stopped the billionaire CEO in her tracks. Johnna's assistant got in between her and the woman as they started pointing fingers and gesticulating wildly, like two ratchet, young, project chicks, and then Johnna launched herself at the much heavier woman. She grabbed a handful of the woman's hair and yanked her head down. She hit her with a couple of uppercuts and clawed her across the face before the assistant and the other woman pulled them apart.

Seven or eight concerned employees spilled out into the hallway to see what all the commotion was about, but McKenzie didn't give them a second look. He zoomed in on the burly woman Johnna had assaulted, studied her bleeding face, and then went to the photo IDs of all the Panteon Tech employees and found her name.

Diana *Caldwell.*

What were the odds of that?

Chapter 25

Dennis Mixon was called Goldie by all who knew him. He was thirty-eight years old, and in his younger years, he'd been a high-ranking member of the Traveling Vice Lords. He was still affiliated, but nowadays, he went to work eight hours a day and came home to his wife, their two young boys, and their Pit Bull Terrier.

He had a third child from a previous relationship, a twenty-year-old. Her name was Nya Lashay Mixon, and she'd been living with her friend, Lacey, since she was seventeen. Tomorrow was her birthday. Knowing that she'd lost her SUV to the impound, an SUV that had well over a hundred thousand miles on the odometer, he'd spent almost four grand on the down payment for the brand-new Jeep Wrangler he planned to gift Nya first thing tomorrow.

But that was before he heard about Nya's alleged involvement in that triple-murder that had taken place on Thomas and Keystone. Word on the street was that Nya had driven the shooter there, and now, the Cold Gang CVLs and the Wicket town TVLs were on her heels.

The time was 8:57 p.m. The sun had completely left the horizon less than five minutes ago, and for the first time in years, Goldie found himself in traffic instead of in bed at this time of night. He was in the passenger seat of his yellow TVL. Lil Head's, matte black, E-class Mercedes, eyeing every vehicle and pedestrian that passed as Lil Head pulled into the gas station at the corner of Leramie and Chicago Avenue.

There were a lot of pedestrians. The Visionary Lounge, one of Chicago's most popular nightclubs, was just across the street from the gas station, and its parking lot was packed. Most of the club-goers were coming and going from the gas station, most of them young and Black, the majority of the men certified gang members just like Goldie and Lil head.

"Call my niece," Lil Head said as he parked next to a gas pump. He'd been calling Nya his niece ever since she was born. "I know she fucked up big time, but this ain't no time to be mad at her. You gotta make sure she a'ight."

Goldie had gotten a text from Nya saying she was okay after her house was shot up, but he'd been far too upset about her involvement in the Keystone Avenue shooting to reply. Now, he FaceTimed her, and he continued to study the faces in the crowd while he waited for her to answer.

"Hey, Daddy," she answered after a couple of rings. There was loud music and even louder conversation in the background. She was in a room with enormous floor-to-ceiling windows; Goldie could see the Chicago skyline through the windows over her shoulder.

"Where you at?" Goldie asked.

"At the Costilla Hotel. It's that nice, new, five-star hotel Alexus Costilla opened downtown. It's sooo nice. We're having, like, a pre-birthday bash before the real turn up tomorrow."

Goldie clenched his teeth, narrowed his eyes, and tilted his head to one side. Reading his body language, Nya shook her head and sighed.

"I know, Daddy," she said. "I swear, all I did was help out a man who got carjacked right in front of me. I told him who did it and let him use my phone, and…"

"*And you drove him over there.* What the fuck was you thinkin'?"

Nya went silent. Of course she had no defense for her actions. She'd gotten in somebody else's business, and now, she had some real deal gangsters on her ass about it.

"Who is this nigga?" Goldie asked when it became apparent that Nya wasn't going to say anything.

"His name is Renz… Grizzy. It's Grizzy."

"Why you start to say Renz?"

"It's a fake name I gave him when I first met him. I called him Renzo. But his name is Grizzy. He's a GD from out south."

"And you gon' let this brick ass nigga getchoo killed out here?!"

The term "brick" was a derogatory name for Gangster Disciples. Goldie had hated GDs for as long as he could remember. He'd been robbed and shot by a group of GDs back in 2007. He'd gone to meet up with a girl at her apartment on 69th and Wolcott, and as soon as he got out of his car, a group of GDs jumped out of a minivan and ran down on him with guns aimed at his head. Unwilling to go out like a sucker, he'd lunged for one of their pistols, and they had shot him three times, once in the shoulder, once in the chest, and once in the stomach. They'd robbed him for his gold necklace, a few grams of dro, and about twenty-four hundred dollars in cash.

Ever since then, it had been *fuck* the GDs.

"He's a good man, Daddy," Nya countered. "You know I don't just go for no anybody. He's a real one. He ain't no pushover either. That's the only reason they mad. They robbed the wrong nigga, and he got they ass like he was s'posed to."

Goldie glanced up at a trio of teenage dreadheads who were walking past the front of the Benz. He recognized two of them as Cold Gang members, Sticks and Nardo, and instinctively, he reached under the right leg of his jeans and closed his hand around the handle of his Smith & Wesson pistol. But the boys paid him no mind. They walked on into the gas station, and Goldie returned his attention back to his daughter's exceptionally pretty face.

"Stay away from the west side for a couple days," he said. "You and Lacey can go stay at your mama's house in Bellwood. Just don't go back to that house on Central. And let me know if you hear about anybody else makin' threats. I'm about to call Sleet and Wobble and holla at these niggas. Let em know you my motherfuckin' daughter. If they still on bullshit after that, I'm whackin' some'n tonight. On King Neal."

"Daddy, go home," Nya pleaded.

"Love you, baby girl," Goldie said and ended the call.

He turned his attention back to the three young dreadheads. They were inside the store. Lil Head was in there too, speaking with the clerk at the counter.

"Bitch ass nigga," Goldie muttered. He looked down at his phone, went to his list of contacts, found Sleet's number, and dialed it.

Chapter 26

Sticks had seen Nya's father sitting in the passenger seat of the black Mercedes, but he didn't mention it to the gang until they were inside the store, their eyes wandering across a rack of potato chips.

Nardo was talking about Coi Leray and Rubi Rose, the cute, young female rappers who were currently performing at The Visionary Lounge, when Stick cut him off mid-sentence.

"Bro, on the gang, that's Nya's pops sittin' in that Benz out there," he said, picking up a bag of ranch flavored Doritos from the rack. "He used to fuck with my auntie when I was a kid. That's how I first met Nya."

Nardo and Blammer both turned their heads to look out the large, square windows, and Sticks immediately smacked Nardo across the head with the bag of Doritos. "And you stupid ass niggas just gon' turn and look," he said, and they turned their attention back to the potato chips.

Blammer's expression went from cool to furious in an instant, and his hand moved toward the waistline of his Reebok joggers. He had great reason to be upset. Keith "Blammer" Green's older, half-brother, Red Rum, had been shot in the arm during the Keystone Avenue shooting earlier today. Blammer had rushed out from beside his great-aunt's house with a Draco and joined the gunfight just as Nya and the mystery gunman were making their getaway in the Nissan Altima, and he'd sworn to Red Rum that, as soon as he saw Nya or any of her kin, he would pull his pistol and open fire.

"Chill, bro," Sticks said as four laughing, young women went sauntering past behind them, one of them pausing to playfully finger flick Nardo's earlobe before continuing on down the aisle. "Not right here. Too many people and it's two police cars sittin' in that McDonald's parking lot right across the street. We'll just hop in the whip and follow em."

"I'ma call Sleet," Nardo said, dialing their gang leader's number on his smartphone.

Sticks took his Doritos and a pack of Jolly Ranchers and got in line behind an older man in an Air Jordan tee shirt and jeans. The man was buying a twenty-ounce Dr. Pepper, a pack of Newport Kings, and gas for his vehicle, and he glanced back at Nardo when Nardo started talking to Sleet.

"Big homie," Nardo said, "we're over here at the gas station on Laramie and Chicago Avenue, and we just ran across Nya's pops. He sittin' in a black Benz out here right now."

Sleet's response came through the speakerphone loud and clear. "Yeah, he just called me. I got him on the other line now. Can't lie, I got a lotta respect for that nigga, but shit, we just lost three shorties today, and we still ain't found out who did it. All we know is who the driver was. We *gotta* change the score. Nya ain't come forward and said nothin', so it's open season."

The term "changing the score" was street lingo for retaliation. If a rival gang killed a member of your gang and in turn your gang murdered one of theirs, then the score was even, and in order to go up on the score (or "change" it), your gang had to murder another member of theirs.

As it stood, Cold Gang was down three, not to mention the others who'd been wounded in the Keystone Avenue shooting, and they had yet to drop a single body in return.

"A'ight," Nardo said, nodding his head and looking out at the matte black Mercedes sedan. "Say no more. We on his ass."

Chapter 27

When Nya returned to the sitting room, Quita and Brielle were twerking in their booty shorts while everyone else sat around the table, drinking and laughing and talking. Nu-Nu's sister, Niecy, had arrived with two other neighborhood girls, and they were rapping along to Big Boss Vette's *Pretty Girl Walk* while Marcus told Lacey about the time some southside gangster named Kut Throat Dre had murdered Chief Keef's Glo Gang artist Capo right in front of Marcus's ex-girlfriend's house.

"And then," Marcus was saying, "right after he whacked Capo, he slid down on my nigga, Crasher, in Englewood and upped a stupid, long ass choppa. Some military type shit. He tried to make folks call one of the other folks over there, so he could whack him next. On Larry, that cock eyed nigga had balls, and that lil stripper bitch, Baldie Bandz, he was fuckin' on was bad as hell."

Five bottles of Dussé had been purchased. There was also a birthday cake, ice cream, hot wings, eight extra large pizzas, THC infused snacks, and several 2-liter bottles of Pepsi. Uptown was passing out Percocet and Roxies like candy, and when Nya caught Grizzy popping two of the Percs, she said fuck it and popped one herself.

There wasn't much room left on the sofa, so for the second time today, Nya found herself settling onto Grizzy's lap. She thought it was the best seat in the room. He closed his powerful arms around her waist and pulled her back against him. He whispered in her ear. "You know you the baddest bitch in here, right?"

Nya's face lit up with a lottery-winning smile. She bit down on her bottom lip, turned back at Grizzy, and said, "You know you my man now, right?"

Grizzy chuckled. "That goes without saying. I was gon' tell you that anyway. You give that pussy to anybody else, they gettin' smoked on sight. On Larry Hoover."

He slipped his hand down between her thighs as he spoke, pressing his fingertips against her pussy. The overwhelming combination of his gangster words and his aggressive touch sent a warm wave of emotion washing through Nya. She blushed and said nothing, listening to the conversation and vibing to the music, sipping from her cup of cognac, and occasionally lifting her phone to check the notifications on her social media pages. She kept getting concerned messages from friends in the Austin neighborhood, who she'd known for years, and she kept replying that she was fine. Surprisingly, she didn't even feel a little worried about Cold Gang and Wicked Town coming after her. Not with Grizzy by her side. He crossed her as the kind of man who would stop at nothing to protect his woman. She had hope that her father would be able to get both gangs to squash the whole issue with her, but if he didn't, she felt confident that Grizzy would keep her safe from harm's way.

And if all else failed, she still had the Glock in her purse.

After a while, the music transitioned from hip hop to R&B. Chris Brown's *Under the Influence* came on, and seconds later, Nu-Nu went over to the wall and dimmed the lights. She was a bad bitch in Nya's opinion, light-skinned and slim with the kind of big, round ass and jutting hips a girl like Nya could only dream of having. Her eyes were green too, like La La Anthony's or Alexus Costilla's, and she was so sexy and sweetly feminine that most men couldn't help but to fall in love with her at first sight.

Nya liked her too. She'd never been intimate with a woman before, but she fantasized about it often enough. She didn't have enough fingers and toes to count the number of times she'd used her vibrator while envisioning herself in a threesome with a fine-ass nigga like Grizzy and a bad ass bitch like Noesha "Nu-Nu" Long.

Normally, Nya would have been much too shy to make such a bold proposition, but she was tipsy from all the weed and liquor, and her twenty-first birthday was just a few hours away, so she was able to dig deep down inside herself and find the courage to wave Nu-Nu over and whisper in her ear.

"You uhh… wanna come in the room with me and Renzo?"

Nya had yet to stop referring to Grizzy as Renzo in front of her friends. She'd used the fake name so many times throughout the day that his own gang had started using the name.

Nu-Nu smirked and nodded her head. Hardly anyone even looked their way as Nya got up and led Grizzy and Nu-Nu toward the bedroom. Lacey was on Marcus's lap, facing him. He'd lifted the front of her Rihanna shirt and was sucking on her titties while rubbing his hands all over her ass. Brielle was on Uptown's lap. Quita was on Smoke's. The sexual tension in the room was thick, and Nya moved hurriedly toward the bedroom, eager to get out of her skintight Ethika outfit and on top of somebody's face.

At that moment, whatever Nya's father was up to was the furthest thing from her mind.

Chapter 28

Due in part to the famous rap artists performing at The Visionary Lounge, traffic in the Austin neighborhood was particularly heavy, and the streets were teeming with police activity, which was only to be expected. With five killed and five wounded in less than eight hours (including the boy who'd arrived at Loretta Hospital with nine gunshot wounds to his legs and upper thighs), the Chicago Police Department had their hands full.

Goldie hated the heavy police presence. He was on the edge of his seat with Lil Head's fifty shot Mac-11 clutched tightly in one hand. The three dreadheads from the gas station were trailing two cars behind in a dark colored Pontiac G6. Goldie had lowered his window and was looking back at them, waiting for the perfect opportunity to either lift his upper body out the window and take aim at the Pontiac or get out of the car and take aim at the Pontiac.

Either way it went, he was certainly going to take aim at the Pontiac.

He'd have done it a few blocks back, on Cortez Street, but a CPD squad car had driven past just as he was getting ready to make his move.

They turned onto the 4700 block of West Maypole Avenue, and then, they went east on Kinzie, and finally, when they reached the stop sign at the intersection of Kinzie and Keeler, Lil Head slowed the Mercedes to a crawl, and Goldie threw open his door and jumped out.

The Pontiac was half a block back when he did it. It screeched to a stop as he raised the Mac-11. Its doors flew open as he squeezed the trigger and sent a spray of bullets across its hood and windshield, and the three boys rushed out with their own guns raised, returning fire as they took cover beside other vehicles that were parked along the curb on both sides of the street.

The flashes of gunfire were blindingly bright, the reports deafening loud. Lil Head ran up beside Goldie, aiming Goldie's .45-caliber Smith & Wesson in both hands. They fired at the three boys, and two of the boys fired back. Meanwhile, the Pontiac began to drift forward in their direction.

"Go that way," Goldie said, motioning to the right side of the street where one of the boys had just fallen over next to a Honda pickup.

Goldie took off running toward the other side of the street where the other two boys were crouched beside a white Chevy Camaro. Goldie was short and stocky, just five and a half feet tall, while Lil Head was six feet even and a bit on the heavier side. Goldie was quick on his feet, Lil Head, not so much. Two flashes of gunfire came from beside the Honda pickup across the street, just as Lil Head stepped onto the curb, and he dropped down on one knee, holding his considerable gut.

Goldie saw it out of the corner of his eye. It threw him off a little, and when he regained focus, it was too late. He fired the Mac-11 at the two dreadheads crouched next to the Camaro half a second after they rose up, firing at him. The bullets felt like Mike Tyson punches hitting his chest, his arm, his scrotum, his thigh, his shoulders, his left hand. He held onto the trigger and kept shooting as the impact of the bullets striking him sent him stumbling backward, and he watched the two boys fall flat on their backs as he fell flat on his.

Quickly — well, as quickly as he could move considering his injuries — Goldie rolled over onto his stomach and army-crawled from the sidewalk to the street. He was only vaguely aware of Lil Head helping him to his feet, and then, the two of them were staggering toward the Mercedes, Lil Head groaning in agony, Goldie gasping for breath and spitting out blood.

Somewhere in the distance, a woman screamed out that her baby had been shot. Goldie was blacking out when he heard it, and when he came to, he was stretched out on the backseat of Lil Head's E350. He blinked, and suddenly, he was in the back of an ambulance with some sort of plastic breathing mask strapped to his face.

"Breathe, sir," the medic looking down at him was saying. "Just breathe. You're gonna make it. You are going to make it…"

He tried to speak, to get the medic to phone his daughter and tell her what had happened, but all that came out was a wet, wheezing sound. Then, his vision went all blurry, and his world went black again.

Chapter 29

Grizzy's triumphant little grin spoke volumes.

He was looking down at the most wonderful sight he could ever remember seeing — two stunningly attractive, young, Black women, both of them butt naked and on all fours, servicing his hard, black dick like there was no tomorrow.

Currently, his dick was in Noesha's possession, the majority of its glistening wet length vanishing and reappearing as she sucked him in and out of her saliva-soaked mouth. (He couldn't think of her as Nu-Nu; that was his Uncle Robert's nickname.) Nya was running one hand over his abs while she held his balls in the other, massaging them with her fingers.

They had been taking turns sucking Grizzy's dick for about ten minutes now. He was watching them do it through the screen of his smartphone, recording video of the event simply because he'd never had, in the famous words of Future, two bad bitches at the same damn time.

He had to stop recording when he got a text message from Malaysia, the thickly built exotic dancer whose boyfriend was his drug connect. She wanted to know if he was ready to re-up. He texted back that he was. He only had three kilos of cocaine and two kilos of heroin left, and he'd already used a brick of fentanyl to stretch the heroin as far as he could without reducing its potency. He was paying $35,000 per kilo of fentanyl, $70,000 per kilo of heroin, and $40,000 per kilo of cocaine. He had no complaints about the prices because Malaysia's boyfriend — Leroy "Bam" Patterson, a gang leader from the west side's North Lawndale neighborhood — had the purest dope in the city, and Grizzy was an expert when it came to using cutting agents to multiply his product. The purer the dope was when he got it, the more he was able to stretch it.

After replying to the text message, Grizzy shut his eyes, set his phone down beside him, and thought about the surprising revelation that Johnna Broward had taken the money from Butch and used it to start her company. The news had made Grizzy even more determined to get his father's money back but knowing that the money was now in Johnna's bank account made things a lot more difficult. Even if she did send Butch the millions of dollars she'd promised him, how was Grizzy going to get Butch to hand it over? Forcing him to transfer that much money would undoubtedly lead to an arrest and a lifelong prison sentence, and the money would be seized long before Grizzy was able to spend even a small percentage of it.

So, what was he to do?

He opened his eyes and picked up his phone. He typed out a text message to his father and sent it then went back to staring smilingly at Nya and Noesha just as Nya threw a leg over him and backed her ass up until her flowery pink pussy was hovering right over his mouth.

"You know what to do, nigga," Nya said, and she was right.

Grizzy put his hands on her waist and went to licking and sucking on her hooded clitoris as she began sucking his dick. His toes curled over when he felt his balls being sucked into the warm cavern of Noesha's wet mouth. If not for the Percocet he'd taken, he knew he would have ejaculated a long time ago. But he'd taken them, and he was ready for battle.

He smacked Nya's ass and pulled her cheeks apart, licking his lips as he watched her beautiful, pink pussy spread open. He spat on her tightly puckered asshole and pushed his forefinger inside it, all the way to the second knuckle, and when she sat back to let Noesha get her turn at sucking him off, he pulled her down onto his mouth and flickered his pointed tongue across the wrinkled brown circle. Like the great Kevin Gates. Her back door hole tightened and relaxed as he did it, and Grizzy decided it didn't taste anywhere near as bad as he'd expected it to be. In fact, there was no real taste at all, just skin and the lingering taste of her vaginal juices on his tongue.

He ventured a little deeper into unchartered territory, pushing his tongue inside of her, and she purred in response to the anal penetration, reaching between her thighs to rub on her clitoris as the wet slab of muscle in Grizzy's mouth brought her to the brink of an orgasm.

She came a short time later. It was a tremendous orgasm that left a string of creamy vaginal juice dangling down in front of Grizzy's chin. He dipped his head down to slurp it up and then spit it onto her shiny, wet asshole as he reached for the box of Magnum condoms on the bedside table.

As Grizzy moved onto his knees, rolling the extra-large rubber onto his long, hard pole of a penis, Noesha turned her ass to him and lowered her head to the plush white comforter. It was an immensely arousing view, her fat, little pussy wedged between her fat, light brown ass. As he eased the head of his dick into Noesha, Nya rose up on her knees and kissed him on the mouth.

"Happy birthday to *me*," she said, cheesing.

Grizzy grinned his handsome grin, smacked Noesha on her left buttock, and watched it wiggle as he started slamming in and out of her. As he fucked her, he was reminded of a line from another popular rap song. This song wasn't performed by Future or anyone else from Future's generation of trap rappers. No, this was a line from a rap song Grizzy had heard on the radio all the time in the early nineties when he was just a kid. Hip-Hop legend Ice Cube had coined the phrase, and Grizzy thought there was no better way to describe his current mood than this — 'I gotta say, today was a good day.'

Chapter 30

Johnny "Bang Boy" Broward was well connected inside the walls of FCI Terre Haute prison. After being transferred from the federal institution's Communication Management Unit in early 2020, he'd had his caseworker —an ill-built, white woman named Mrs. Knox, who was married to a verbally abusive meth addict and was madly in love with Johnny — pull some strings to get him moved into the same cell as Willie White, his longtime mentor. The smartphone he'd paid Mrs. Brown $5,000 to smuggle in to him was stuffed down inside his mattress when he moved into the cell with Willie, but his charger had broken, so he'd used Willie's cell phone charger until he found another one for sale.

Johnny's younger sister, Johnna, had deposited $2.5 million into his prison account three years ago, which allowed him to spend a few hundred dollars on commissary food every week. As a result, he and Willie usually spent most of their time in the cell either eating huge meals or exercising to sweat out the excess calories.

Even so, the two men were huge, their tall, brown bodies packed full of rock-hard muscle. Willie was fifty-six years old, but he looked twenty years younger. He was 6'4" and two hundred fifty-eight pounds with zero percent body fat. Johnny was similarly built, 6'2" and a few pounds lighter than Willie. The two of them were at the top of the food chain. They had an iron grip on the prison's drug trade, thanks in part to the additional $2.5 million Johnna had wired to an online bank account that Johnny accessed from his illegal cell phone.

There was only one Black female guard at the prison. Her name was Shanelle Boatman, and she was originally from Decatur, Georgia. Johnny had offered her $20,000 to become his mule. Three days later, she'd slipped him a note, saying she was game. He had used the Zelle banking app to send her the money, and on her first trip in, she'd brought him a sausage shaped package containing four ounces of meth and one thousand Suboxone strips. He'd made $200,000 off the Suboxone alone, selling each of the small orange rectangles for $200. The ice had gone for $350 a gram, so he'd made close to forty thousand dollars off the four ounces. Not that he'd needed the money. He'd only made the move to aid his brothers, the federal inmates who were loyal members of the Almighty Black P. Stone Nation.

Ms. Boatman had smuggled in two more packages this morning, and Johnny had really loaded her up this time — three ounces of heroin, two ounces of cocaine, six ounces of meth, two hundred Roxicodone pills, and eleven hundred more Suboxone strips.

But Johnny wasn't thinking about the packages right now nor was he thinking about the two Aryan Brotherhood members three of his own gang members had stabbed up over a poker game last night. His only concern at the moment was Johnna Broward, which was why he was on his top bunk with his thin, white blanket pulled over his head and his iPhone held up in front of his face.

"Why didn't you tell me you had hired that fuckin' rat?" Johnny asked through clenched teeth as he studied his sister's noticeably battered face on his phone screen. Mrs. Knox had brought him the AirPod buds he had in his ears. He was doing his best to whisper; it was a quarter past midnight, and down on the bottom bunk, his cellmate, Willie White, was fast asleep.

"I didn't know it was him," Johnna said. She paused to lick the stitched corner of her bottom lip. "Butch talked me into hiring him, and I just didn't think to check and see who he was. I mean, I knew he had just gotten out of prison, and that he was one of the White Moes, but that was it."

The "White Moes" was the unofficial nickname of the Black P. Stones who'd terrorized the Altgeld Gardens neighborhood under Willie White's leadership. Most Black P. Stones were called Moes because of their close ties to the Moroccan community, so the name White Moes had come about naturally.

"That man ain't no Moe. He's a rat, the whole reason I'm in prison now. And you shouldn't have been talkin' to Butch in the first place. He's another rat, and you can't say you didn't know that."

"I couldn't just cut him off after I stole twenty-three million dollars from him, now could I? I tried that when I first took the money, and Butch came after me. He showed up at every Panteon press event. When we opened the building in Lower Manhattan, he was right there in the lobby that first week. He caught me leaving out with my assistant and threatened to go to the police if I didn't repay him in full. I sent him a million dollars, and I thought that would be enough to keep him quiet for a while."

"And obviously it didn't."

"No, it didn't. He kept pestering me, and then, he got a hold of my private email address and started messaging me about hiring Caldwell, saying it was the least I could do after what I'd done to him. When I finally did hire Caldwell, he didn't give off any negative vibes. He was so approachable. He was always the brightest light in the room. Always on time. He ended up dating one of our accountants, and they got married six weeks later. Had I known that Butch had sent him to figure out what I'd done with the money, and that he would go nuts on us after we fired him for snooping around in my office, I'd have never hired him from the start."

Johnna held her hand up to the camera. Two of her fingernails were broken off.

"What happened to your fingernails?" Johnny asked.

"I had to put hands on Caldwell's fat ass wife this morning. The bitch gon' walk past me and mutter something about me firing her husband. Come to think of it, that might've been what set him off. She probably called him after our fight."

"You can't be puttin' hands on people like that. You're a billionaire. She could sue you."

"That bitch ain't gon' sue me." Johnna yawned and winced when her mouth stretched open a little too widely and strained her stitches. She switched to her phone's rear camera and showed Johnny the sky-high view from her Streeterville penthouse. "Look at this view. It's so pretty from way up here. Especially at night."

"Hell yeah. It's beautiful." Johnny's lungs seemed to tighten, and a wave of melancholy washed over him as he remembered all the glorious nights he'd spent in Chicago. "Damn, I miss the city."

"Look over there." She pointed toward a row of skyscrapers in the distance. "That tall building in the middle is the new Costilla Hotel and Tower. That bitch, Alexus Costilla, is worth over two hundred *billion* now." She switched back to the front camera and gazed at Johnny with a look of pure wonderment in her eyes. "You know, the lawyer I hired for you — and for me too — is also Alexus Costilla's lawyer. Her whole law firm is working on your appeal right now, and she said it looks promising. She told me the other day to expect to be seeing you home sometime next year."

Johnny smiled, and another overwhelming feeling washed over him.

This one wasn't melancholy.

It was hope.

Chapter 31

Crunchy's jaw was broken in three different places. The surgeon had numbed his mouth before wiring his jaw back together, but the numbing medication had worn off hours ago. He'd gone home to change clothes and returned to Loretta Hospital even angrier than he'd been earlier because he hadn't realized the five grand was missing from his pocket until he was taking off his blood-stained clothes in the bathroom at his mother's apartment.

He had taken an Uber back to the hospital, and now, he was standing outside the hospital's side entrance, smoking a cigarette even though the surgeon had warned him against it, looking down at his smartphone with a cantankerous scowl on his face.

The date on his phone screen had switched over to May 24. He'd received a Facebook notification that today was Nya Mixon's twenty-first birthday, and now, he was on her page, glaring daggers at the well wishes.

"Excuse me, can I get a light?"

The young woman's voice startled Crunchy, and he turned to look back at her as she came walking out of the glass sliding doors. He immediately recognized her as Nataya, a relatively pretty, young, hood chick he'd known for years. She wore a blood-spotted, blue tee shirt over tight blue jeans and Jordan 11 sneakers. A few inches of her gut bulged out over a Gucci belt buckle that looked like it had seen better days.

When she realized it was him, her eyelids moved close together.

"I ain't have nothin' to do with that shit," he said, offering her his cigarette lighter. "I sold the nigga that car, and he went over there with Nya and did that bullshit. I was at the crib with Lacey." His nostrils flared when he spoke Lacey's name. "I'ma kill *both* of them bitches. That nigga too."

Reluctantly, Nataya accepted the lighter and put fire to the end of her cigarette. She inhaled and stared out into the parking lot, shaking her head in disbelief.

"Bianca's paralyzed," she said, her eyes still on the parking lot. "The bullet went right through the middle of her spine."

"My lil brother in there fucked up too. Lacey shot him nine times."

Nataya gasped and turned to look at him. "Lacey shot *Curry*?" She narrowed her eyes again and furrowed her brow "And what the fuck happened to your mouth?"

Too embarrassed to state the truth, Crunchy said, "I fell and broke my shit on the table when she started shootin'. Knocked myself out. When I woke up, lil bro was layin' there, all shot up, and that big bitch was gone with both of our pistols and all of my money."

Nataya's jaw muscles flexed repeatedly. Her nostrils mimicked Crunchy's. She went back to looking out into the parking lot, shaking her head again, glowering.

"Somebody gotta do somethin' to them bitches," she said finally. "Do you know how many people done got shot since all that shit went down this mornin'? The police caught Tavaris and somebody else from Cold Gang after they shot up Nya and Lacey's house over there on Central. Tavaris pointed his gun at the cops, and they shot him and the nigga he had with him. Then, Sticks, Blammer, and Nardo just got hit up somewhere on Keeler. Blammer said they shot up Nya's daddy and one of his guys, but I guess they was shootin' back, so everybody ended up shot. Nardo didn't make it. And *none* of this would've happened if Nya hadn't taken ol' boy over to our house in the first place. Somebody need to kill that bitch."

"I'd do it myself if I had a gun," Crunchy said, blowing smoke out of his nose. "And the bitch stole all my bread, so I can't even go and buy one. Now, I'ma be into it with Cold Gang over this bullshit, and I…"

"No, I got'choo," Nataya said, shaking her head again. "I still got that money Mikey n'em took from that nigga. He gave me and Bee twenty-five hundred apiece. I'll buy you a gun. One of my baby daddies is from Indianapolis, and he sells guns. He's already coming to pick up his son in the morning. I'll have him bring me a gun when he comes, and I'll just buy it and give it to you. Long as you promise to use it to kill Nya's ass, you can have it."

Crunchy looked up at her. The nod he gave her this time was more vehement than the last one "I heard you," he said. "You gon' buy the pipe from your baby daddy, and you want me to use it to whack Nya." He raised his phone and showed her the brief shot of Lacey and Nya in the background. "And I know some hoes who'll lead me right to her."

Chapter 32

When Johnna awakened at precisely 5:59 a.m. to the welcoming aroma of freshly brewed coffee, she wrapped a silk, Gucci bathrobe around her naked body, tied it at the waist, and picked up her phone and laptop computer before heading down to the kitchen, this time using the elevator instead of the glass staircase.

She found her mother sitting at the glass top table, drinking a mug of coffee and reading something on her iPhone that had her smiling from ear to ear.

"Go on and sit down," April Broward said, getting up. "I'll get you a pastry and make you some coffee."

"The hell are you so happy about at six o'clock in the morning?" Johnna asked as she sat down across the table from her mother's seat and lifted the lid on her computer.

"You'll see. Trust me, Johnna, *you will see.* Google Panteon on your computer. Or just go to any news site. I'm sure it'll be the top story."

Johnna turned on her MacBook Pro and found dozens of new emails, but she didn't click on any of them. She went to The Wall Street Journal website, just like she'd done every morning since her company's initial public offering in early March, and what she found in bold lettering at the top of the front page brought an impossibly wide smile to her sleepy, brown face.

PANTEON TECH STOCKS SOAR!

Johnna gasped, glanced at her beaming mother with wide eyes, and turned back to read the news article.

'Following yesterday's deadly shooting at Panteon Tech headquarters in Lower Manhattan, investors have rallied together in support of the shooting victims, purchasing billions of dollars in Panteon stocks and sending the company to the forefront of the New York Stock Exchange. In mere hours, Panteon CEO Johnna Broward's net worth has skyrocketed from $2.8 billion to a staggering $8.9 billion while the price of Panteon shares has risen from $31.80 to $94.22.

And the buck doesn't stop there. Panteon products have been flying off the shelves at Walmart, Target, and Home Depot, and six of the top ten bestsellers in Amazon's electronics department are from Panteon Technologies.

Some believe that a supportive Instagram post from billionaire tycoon Alexus Costilla — who recently surpassed Selena Gomez and Kylie Jenner to become the most followed woman on the platform with over four hundred seventeen million followers — may have played a role in Panteon's unprecedented boost in stock sales, but whatever the case may be, the fact remains that the innocent lives lost in yesterday's shooting has galvanized consumers and investors more than anyone could have possibly foreseen...'

Johnna picked up her iPhone and went to Instagram, intent on hurrying over to see Alexus Costilla's page to view the supportive post for herself. But as it turned out, she wouldn't even need to go to her idol's page. The Shade Room had already shared the post, and it was the first video Johnna saw on her Instagram feed.

It was a two-part video. The first part showed Alexus (or "Queen A" as most Black Americans referred to her) purchasing over a billion dollars' worth of Panteon stock on her own MacBook Pro while a crowd of her family and friends, including her billionaire rap star husband Blake "Bulletface" King, stood applauding behind her. The second part showed Alexus inside a Target store somewhere in Brownsville, Texas, gifting surprised shoppers free Panteon Tech home security systems. And not the cheaper ones either. The Panteon Home Fortress Pro was $849.99, and Alexus had nine carts full of them.

The two-part video had Johnna wanting to cry and leap for joy at the same time, but she didn't actually do it until she went to the short list of pages Alexus was following and saw that her page had joined the list.

Johnna's chair tipped over backwards as she jumped up, threw her head back, and screamed to the top of her lungs.

"Mmm hmm." April snickered. "And just to let you know, I got Kurt Rappaport on speed dial. As soon as you calm down, I'ma need you to get him on the phone and see if you can't get your mama one of those two-hundred-million-dollar Malibu mansions like the one he just sold Jay and Bey."

"Whatever you want, Mama," Johnna said with tears of joy streaming down her cheeks.

April brought over a coffee and a cheese Danish on a napkin, but Johnna was too overwhelmed with emotion to ingest much of anything.

She sat back in her chair, pressed her hands to her face, and cried.

Chapter 33

Nya Mixon sat forward in her seat, buried her face in the palms of her hands, and cried.

It was 6:42 a.m., the morning of her twenty-first birthday, and she had just turned her phone on to find a bunch of text messages from several of her family members saying her father had been shot sometime last night and so had his close friend, Lil Head. They had been transported to separate hospitals with Lil Head going to Loretta and Goldie being airlifted to the University of Chicago Medical Center's trauma unit in Hyde Park.

Nya felt terrible. Sick to her stomach. She'd turned off her phone to let it charge before last night's threesome and hadn't turned it back on until a few minutes ago when they were dropping off Smoke and Uptown at the apartment building on 78th and Paulina. Now, she was alone in the Trackhawk with Grizzy, shuddering and shaking and sobbing, while Grizzy rubbed his hand up and down her back and drove.

She tried to think clearly and failed quite horribly. Her mind was in shambles, and the one question that kept coming to her was "Did my daddy get shot because of me?"

When they made it in the gated community where Grizzy lived on 81st and Prairie, Nya hardly even noticed the sleek, black Audi SUV that had parked in the driveway. The tall goddess from Grizzy's ex, Joya Kelly's, IG page — the one Nya had suspected was their daughter — stood barefoot on the second step of the staircase in the foyer, wrapped in a hot-pink, Fendi bathrobe, holding a small, white French bulldog in one arm and a sweating can of Mountain Dew in the other hand. Nya practically ignored her, as she gave a simple wave and a teary-eyed hint of a smile, and then she had Grizzy show her to his bedroom where she curled up in his huge bed with two pillows in her arms, closed her eyes, and cried some more.

Grizzy stepped just outside the bedroom door and spoke with his daughter. He called her Kamari, and he mentioned Nya's name more than once, but Nya couldn't make out much more than that. She wasn't trying to. She was still trying to wrap her head around what had happened to her father. Everything else was background noise.

She was aware of a sudden complete silence when both Grizzy and Kamari left from outside the bedroom doorway. A few minutes later, she heard the distinctive thumps of Grizzy's approaching foot falls, and she opened her bloodshot eyes to find him re-entering the room with her suitcase and the two grocery bags she'd put all her shoes in.

He came over and took her face in his hands, kissed her once on the forehead, and again on the lips.

"I got a few runs to make," he said. "I'll be back in an hour or so, and if you want, we can go straight to the hospital to see your old man. Or you can just take one of my other cars or have Kamari drive you over there. It's up to you."

She nodded weakly.

"The bathroom's right across the hall. Kamari has her own bathroom upstairs, so if you need any of that girl stuff, just ask her. You know where the kitchen is, and she already made breakfast. Feel free to eat whenever you're ready."

Another weak nod from Nya.

"You need anything before I go?"

"Just a water," she replied, just as weakly. *And another one of those kisses*, she thought to herself. That warm kiss on the lips had strengthened her a little, caused a notable stirring in her heart's core, but she felt that requesting another one would be wrongfully selfish considering the fact that her father was laid up in a trauma center, likely because of her.

But she wouldn't need to ask. Grizzy went out to the kitchen and returned with a cold bottled water, and he gave her another invigorating kiss, this time holding his incredibly soft lips against hers for a good five seconds before turning to leave.

The spirit-lifting strength she gained from those two smooches gave her enough courage to pick up her phone and read the other text messages. Goldie had no siblings, but Lil Head's adult children were essentially blood relatives to the Mixon family, and all four of them had messaged Nya about the shooting. So had Christine, Nya's mother, and Goldie's wife, Tasha. The only news they had about the shooting was the version Lil Head had given them, that he and Goldie had been followed from the gas station by three young boys with dreads and they had gotten into a shootout on Kinzie and Keeler. That was important to know, but Nya needed more.

It was the text message from Lacey that gave her the information she was looking for.

'It was Cold Gang. Blammer, Sticks, and that lame-ass nigga Bernard who was with Derrick and Mikey when he took us to that concert the night Exie broke down. They called him Nardo or whatever. Anyway, he died, Blammer got shot twice and is already out of the hospital, and Sticks is on life support. He got shot once in the head and four times in the chest and stomach. They saying he might die too. Blammer said they followed yo' daddy and Lil Head from that gas station across from The Visionary Lounge, and he say Goldie hopped out on them with a "mack" (whatever tf that is). Blammer told Quita's lil brother the whole story, and she just called and told me. Anyway, I'm @ my mama's house out south. Call me when you get yourself together.'

Nya replied with a simple 'OK' and a sad face emoji. She cracked open her water and took a small swallow. She called her stepmother and learned that her father had six bullet wounds and had just been taken out of his room for a second surgery. Afterward, she shuddered, shut her eyes, and did her best to focus on her breathing and nothing else.

Inhale. Exhale. Inhale. Exhale. Inhale. Exhale...

The breathing method worked.

Three minutes later, she was dreaming.

Chapter 34

Grizzy and his drug connect both lived on 81st and Prairie. Leroy "Bam" Patterson, the connect, had the biggest house on the street with a blacked-out Rolls Royce Cullinan and an Escalade ESV of the same color parked in his driveway. But aside from driving past it every now and then, Grizzy had never visited the place. He always met up with Bam's girlfriend, Malaysia, in the parking lot of the Aldi's on Cottage Grove, and today was no different.

He pulled up alongside her triple-black Escalade, and she got in beside him. They swapped Aldi's bags, and she got out and drove away as if nothing had happened.

Grizzy opened the bag and found three kilos of cocaine, two kilos of heroin, and a kilo of fentanyl. He closed the bag, tossed it onto the backseat and drove to 7013 South Bishop Street, where he spent over an hour pent up in the sparsely furnished apartment with Marcus, their uncle, Robert "Nu-Nu" White, and their four cousins, Jigg, Carleone, Shan-Shan, and Joe-Joe. Grizzy and Marcus used two large pots to cook the two kilos of powder cocaine into eighty-six ounces of crack, and Marcus and the other cousins got to work, measuring and bagging a half kilo of the crack cocaine into $5, $10, and $20 quantities. Grizzy and Nu-Nu began blending the heroin and fentanyl with another cutting agent, and within the hour, the three kilograms of heroin and fentanyl were turned into six and a half kilos of fentanyl-laced heroin.

Grizzy fronted his uncle, Nu-Nu, one of the diluted kilos for $65,000 because Nu-Nu knew a white man with an Audi dealership in Battle Creek, Michigan who was willing to pay $80,000 for it. Carleone and Jigg, who were brothers like Shan-Shan and Joe-Joe, had recently robbed a bank in Aurora, Illinois and made off with over three hundred grand, so it came as no surprise that each of them bought a kilo of the fentanyl-laced heroin from Grizzy. Out of the whole group, only Grizzy and Marcus were GDs. Uncle Nu-Nu was a Traveling Vice Lord, and the others were all Four Corner Hustlers. Not that their gang affiliations really mattered. Family came first, simple as that.

Grizzy ended up selling Marcus the third brick of cocaine for $43,000; it was only a $3,000 profit, but he didn't mind because he knew Marcus would make a good $75,000 at their spot on 72nd and Green, and Marcus was by far his favorite cousin. Shan-Shan and Joe-Joe both agreed to take the day's supply of crack and heroin to Grizzy's other two drug spots. They'd each get $2,000 for helping bag up the dope and delivering it to Grizzy's workers. Grizzy put the remainder of his dope in a black duffel bag and made a phone call, and minutes later, his cousin, Michele, arrived to pick up the duffel bag and stash it at her place on 56th and Michigan.

When all was said and done, Grizzy went out and sat in his Trackhawk, drinking from a lukewarm bottle of Fiji water and listening to an old Gucci Mane song on the radio, while pondering over the chaos he'd brought into Nya's life. When Marcus joined him in the truck a few minutes later, Grizzy looked over at his cousin and shook his head.

"What?" Marcus said. "What the fuck wrong witchoo?"

"Nya's pops got hit up somewhere out west last night. I knew it had some'n to do with what I did over there. Them niggas on her ass now, all 'cause of me."

"So, what we gon' do about it?"

Grizzy shrugged. He had no answer to that. Now that he knew the money Butch had stolen from his father was no longer in Butch's possession, and that Butch was on his way to Brazil, there was no real reason to go back out west. Not unless Grizzy was going to help Nya retaliate against whoever had shot her father.

"You like shorty, don't you?" Marcus asked. "That lil, bad ass bitch got you whipped already."

Grizzy nodded. "I ain't gon lie. I like her."

"I *know* you like her if you got her at the crib like that." Marcus lowered his window a crack and lit a Newport. "You know I'm witchoo, cuzzo. Whatever you on, I'm on. Shit, I'm tryna wife her thick ass friend anyway. That big, thick muhfucka sucked my dick so good last night. On fo'nem grave, I ain't even wanna drop that bitch off. I already texted shorty and told her I'm pickin' her right back up later on today."

"Ain't nothin' short about that tall ass bitch," Grizzy said with a quick chuckle.

"*Man.* She damn near the same height as *me.* She six two. I had them long ass legs all in the air, on fo'nem." Marcus was smiling hard. He flicked the ash off his cigarette and then lowered the visor mirror to study his reflection.

Up ahead, a dreadheaded boy of about sixteen and a fat girl, who looked to be around the same age, came walking out the front door of a house near the corner. The boy's eyes were everywhere at once, his head swiveling left and right like a bored man in an office chair. Grizzy and Marcus watched him.

"So, what's the deal with Butch?" Marcus asked and pulled his Glock from inside the waistline of his Balmain jeans. "You think he tellin' the truth about Johnna?"

Nodding his head, Grizzy drew his own Glock pistol. It was the look on the fat girl's face that made him do it. She had one hand stuck down in a tall can of Pringles, but she looked deathly afraid, as if she knew something bad was about to happen. Both Grizzy and Marcus turned in their seats to look around, but there was no one else on the street.

"It kinda make sense," Grizzy said. "You know Bang Boy is Johnna's big brother. That nigga was my pop's right-hand man. Shit, he still is. They're in the same cell at FCI Terre Haute. Butch said Bang Boy sent Johnna at him, and she stole the money and used it to start Panteon. And look at what happened yesterday. Panteon got shot up by that old nigga, Mike, the one who used to drive my daddy around all the time. Too many coincidences. I think what happened was Mike tried to get that money out of Johnna, and when she ain't give it up, he said fuck it and started killin' niggas."

"Man," Marcus said, pulling out his phone. "Yo' mama just shared a news link on Facebook that said Johnna Broward's net worth shot up to almost nine billion after that shit went down yesterday. Everybody been buyin' Panteon cameras. They got all kinds of famous people postin' videos in support of Panteon. Doja Cat. Alexus Costilla. Rihanna. Shauni O'Neal. Everybody and they mama buyin' that shit. If that company got started off Uncle Willie's money, then Johnna owes you a whole lot more than thirty Ms."

Grizzy nodded his head in agreement. "Let me get outta here. I gotta go check on shorty. Tell Michele to collect that bread from everybody and bring it to me. I'll be at the crib."

As Marcus was getting out, Grizzy turned to him and added, "Pick up Lacey and bring her over there when you get a minute. Tell her Nya's goin' through it. She might need a friend over there with her."

"Say less," Marcus said and closed the door. He was obviously excited to have a reason to slide on Lacey again.

As Grizzy was driving off, he glanced at the two frightened teenagers. They were rushing off down the sidewalk, and Grizzy figured one of them must have disrespected the wrong person.

That made Grizzy think of Nya and the west side gangsters who were going after her for something *he'd* done.

Sure, she had volunteered to drive him over there, but they weren't upset about her being the getaway driver. They were upset about their homies being dead, and *Grizzy* was responsible for their deaths.

So, he decided it would be Grizzy who ended it. He would track down the heads of the gangs that were after Nya, and he would step on them like brake pedals. And if Nya wanted some get back for what had happened to her father, then Grizzy would show her how to step with him.

Chapter 35

At exactly 10:17 a.m. Eastern Time, Diana Martin-Caldwell looked up at the clock on her living room wall and made the decision that she was going to kill herself as soon as the long hand reached the half-hour mark.

The distraught, young widow was pacing back-and-forth in the East Brooklyn apartment she and her new husband had moved into just thirty-four days ago, drinking from a cup of Crown Royal-laced coffee with tears cascading down her face, occasionally stopping to look at the television.

She was tuned in to MTN News Morning show. Hosts Shameika Hughes and Lequan Foxworthy were discussing the unprecedented boost in Panteon sales and the breaking news that Johnna Broward had actually grown up around Michael Caldwell's dangerous street gang in a housing complex on Chicago's far south side. That made even more tears fall, stinging the scratch marks on the right side of Diana's chubby face.

"I am so sorry, Michael," Diana muttered to the spirit of her dearly departed husband. She sniffled and wiped her nose with a damp ball of tissue. "I should have believed you. I should have *fucking* believed you!"

Michael had given her the backstory of Johnna Broward's improbable rise from rags to riches on the night of their honeymoon, which had ironically been paid for by Johnna Broward.

"She ain't as clean as you think she is," Michael had said as they sat across from each other at a table inside West Hollywood's world-famous Dan Tana's restaurant. His smoldering brown eyes had stared unwaveringly into hers as he said it. "A long time ago, back when I was just a dumb, young nigga with Jeff Fort dreams, I ran with a gang called the Black P. Stones. We were ruthless, and Johnna was right there in the thick of it. She was just a little girl, probably doesn't even remember much of it, but she was there when we had a grip on the south side of Chicago. And you know what? It was the money that *we* made that started Panteon. That mystery $22 million the IRS got on her ass about? Yeah. That came from us."

Diana hadn't believed him then, but she believed him now. It seemed like the whole world had turned against her husband in the past twenty-four hours, but in Diana's opinion, he'd had every right to go after Johnna. Not only had the conceited, young billionaire fired him for snooping around her office in search of the millions of dollars *he* had helped the Black P. Stones accumulate, but then, she'd had the audacity to assault his wife for commenting on his firing.

"That's it. That's the last goddamn straw," Michael had said when Diana FaceTimed him to tell him about the fight with Johnna and to show him the wet, red claw marks on the side of her face. He'd hung up on her, and he hadn't answered the phone when she called back.

A little over an hour later, chaos had erupted as Michael walked up on security guard Romero Alvarez and shot him in the head from point-blank range.

Looking around her living room, Diana sneered at the complete disarray. FBI agents had descended on her apartment in droves shortly after the shooting. They had tossed her bedroom. They had rummaged through every drawer, every trash can, every shoe box. They had confiscated Diana's MacBook computer, and her iPad, and Michael's iPhone. They had taken three boxes of 5.56-

millimeter rifle ammunition from the shelf in Diana and Michael's bedroom closet and the empty rifle case he'd left open on the bed.

Making things worse were the news reporters. CNN. MTN. Fox. ABC. CBS. MSNBC. They were all staked out on the street out front, patiently awaiting Diana's exit, so they could bombard her with the same questions their colleagues had bombarded her with on her way into the building.

"Mrs. Caldwell, did you get a chance to speak with your husband before the shooting?"

"Mrs. Caldwell, were you present during the shooting?"

"Mrs. Caldwell, have you spoken to Johnna Broward?"

Mrs. Caldwell this. Mrs. Caldwell that. And not one question about how Mrs. Caldwell was feeling after losing her husband, after losing four co-workers.

Diana downed the rest of her alcoholic coffee and shot another glance at the clock. 10:25 a.m. In five minutes, she would give those nosey reporters some real news to chow on. The blue steel, .44 Bulldog revolver on her end table was loaded with just two hollow-tipped rounds. This was more than enough seeing as she'd only need one. She'd purchased the firearm following the recent rise in subway attacks, since that was the method of transportation she sometimes used to get to work. She'd had the gun in her purse during the FBI raid, and although one of the federal agents had questioned her extensively, they'd allowed her the dignity of keeping her purse closed during the invasive search of her apartment.

She picked up the revolver and crossed the room to sit in Michael's black, leather recliner. There was a suicide note on the coffee table. In it, she apologized to her two adult sons and her seventeen-year-old, who'd left before the raid to stay with her father. The kids would be alright. Diana's oldest son and his wife owned a successful funeral business, and her other son had recently opened his second barber shop in Queens. They'd take good care of their little sister.

10:28.

Diana closed her eyes and breathed in deeply. She brought the barrel of the gun up to her mouth and parted her lips, tilted her head back, and cleared her mind. Killing herself would be easy like Sunday morning. Especially with the knowledge that Michael would likely be standing there, on the other side, awaiting her arrival. She was just opening her eyes to check the time when someone knocked at her front door. The knock startled her. She stuffed the gun down in the side of the recliner, got up, and turned the suicide note over.

"Yeah? Who is it?" Diana shouted at the door.

"Detective Rick McKenzie, NYPD." A white man shouted back.

Diana took about nine steps toward the door and stopped. There was a mirror on the hallway wall. She turned to it and encountered a beautiful, big-boned, Black woman in distress. Her previously impeccable hairdo was disheveled. She was missing one false eyelash. Her nose was a little swollen, and the scratches on the right side of her face were shiny with antibacterial ointment. A few drops of blood dotted the collar of her beige, silk blouse, and one of the buttons had popped off in the midst of yesterday's scuffle with Johnna. She hadn't showered since yesterday morning.

She sighed, straightened her hair to the best of her ability, and walked the last four or five feet to her door. She unlocked the deadbolt and the doorknob and pulled it open.

"Nasty scratches you got there," the silver-haired cop said, flashing his badge before clipping it back to his waist.

His partner was a stern-faced, Black woman with long, curly hair. She smelled good and looked dangerous, like barbed wire dipped in honey. She had a badge on her waist too, but she didn't flash it. The gun on her hip was bigger than her partner's.

"I'm Detective Sinclair," she said, and that was all.

"Can I help you?" Diana asked, one hand on the door, the other on her hip.

"Yeah," McKenzie said. "You can. You can help us and yourself by filing a police report and pressing charges against Johnna Broward. And if you play your cards right and hire a good attorney, you may be able to come out of this with forty or fifty million dollars for your troubles. It's up to you."

Chapter 36

At exactly ten o'clock in the morning, Central Standard Time, Crunchy found himself sitting in the passenger seat of Nataya's small, gray Ford Focus, which she'd parked in front of Mariah's Salon, just off the corner of Chicago Avenue and Central, while she ran inside to get a quick gel manicure. She'd left her two-year-old son, MJ, in the car with him; the little guy was back there in his car seat, asking a hundred annoying questions, while Crunchy sat staring down at his phone, scrolling through social media and continuing his research on Nya's close-knit group of friends.

"Ay, man," the little boy said. "Why you um... Why yo' name Crunchy? Is it the same like a ummm... like a potato chip? Huh? Like a potato chip?"

"Some'n like that," Crunchy replied dismissively. He had his seat reclined as far back as it could go because he knew that if any member of Cold Gang were to walk or ride past and see him sitting up inside the car, they would likely pull a gun and open fire on him right then and there. No questions asked.

He was currently watching another video on Brielle's Facebook page. This one showed Nya, Lacey, the man she called Renzo, and several other young, Black men and women seated around what looked like a large hotel suite. There were tall windows overlooking downtown Chicago, plush, leather furniture, and an enormous widescreen television. The table in front of the sofas was strewn with bottles of Dussé and Hennessey, paper plates with slices of pizza and chicken wings on them, a few handguns with long, extended clips, and the blue, leather purse that Crunchy recognized as the one Nya had grabbed before she left out with Renzo.

Nya was on Renzo's lap, and the big man had one hand wedged between her thighs, rubbing her there while she drank from a blue plastic cup and smiled like a kid at the candy store. The man, whose lap Lacey was on, looked a lot like Renzo, so much so that Crunchy believed they had to be brothers. Or at least cousins.

"That's a hotel room," Crunchy muttered aloud to himself. Instinctively, his eyes shot up to the top of his phone screen, and he saw that it was ten o'clock on the dot. The video had been posted late last night which meant the group had likely already checked out of whatever hotel they'd partied in.

He shut off his phone screen and sat up for a quick look around before lying back again. The doctor had given him a bottle of liquid Roxicodone for the pain in his jaw, and he'd taken three times the recommended amount before leaving out this morning. He didn't feel a thing.

"Is my daddy here yet?" MJ asked. "Him was s'posed to be here to pick me up, but him not here." He said it as if it was the most shocking betrayal in human history.

Crunchy chuckled twice. "He'll be here, lil man. Me and your mama talked to him a lil while ago. He knows to meet us right here."

MJ's father, whose nickname was Kenwood (which Nataya had explained was the Indianapolis neighborhood he'd grown up in), was bringing a fully automatic pistol that was essentially a miniature AR-15 with a one hundred twenty round drum magazine. He was only charging Nataya $1,000 for the illegally modified weapon. She'd taken the cash out of the cheap, yellow purse, that was currently resting on the driver's seat, and handed it to Crunchy before she headed into the salon. She and Crunchy had FaceTimed with Kenwood less than twenty minutes ago, and Kenwood had flashed the AR-15 pistol in front of the camera before sticking it back into his backpack.

And when Crunchy sat up to take another look around, he saw a lime green Lexus SUV on large chrome rims pull over and park right behind Nataya's car. Crunchy took the thousand dollars Nataya had given him out of his pocket as he watched her baby daddy get out of the Lexus with a backpack strapped to both shoulders, and Crunchy lifted the back of his seat as Kenwood opened the door behind his and got in.

Crunchy pulled the hood of his black, Givenchy hoodie over his dreads as he turned to shake hands with Kenwood. It was his favorite hoodie, purchased with money from a bogus PPP loan he'd gotten during the height of the Covid-19 pandemic.

MJ got really animated when his daddy got in next to him. Kenwood was about 5'10" and chubby, brown-skinned, and dressed in Givenchy from head to toe, only his Givenchy was a lot newer than Crunchy's. He had gold teeth and a diamond necklace. The pendant hanging from his necklace depicted the letters G.S.G. in twinkling white diamonds.

"How you what?" Kenwood said, accepting the cash from Crunchy. He started counting it. "Be careful with this chopper. I just wet a nigga up two days ago with this bitch. One o'dem punk ass Ratchet Boys."

Crunchy furrowed his brow. "Ratchet Boys? The fuck is that?"

"Some Nap Town shit. My clique into it with them niggas. I'm G.S.G., Goon Squad Gorillas. We been beefin' with this lil nigga named Shamus and his clique, the Ratchet Boys. Me and my lil niggas aired em out behind the fairgrounds two days ago." He shrugged and waved it off and kept counting. "I know you ain't tryna hear about no nother nigga city. You prob'ly at war with some niggas out here in the Raq, huh?"

"Yesterday," Crunchy said, nodding, "six bodies got dropped right here in this neighborhood. That's why you see all these police everywhere. And all that shit started over me sellin' somebody a stolen car."

"Yeah, Taya told me about how her sister got shot and three niggas got killed right in front of her house. My son was right there in the front yard when it happened. That's why I'm here to get him now." Kenwood raised his hips off the seat to slip the cash in his pocket then removed the backpack from his shoulders and handed it forward to Crunchy.

"I seen that man shoot my auntie," MJ said. "Him had a shirt on him head, and, and, and him shot Mikey like bam bam bam!"

"You ain't see nothin'," Kenwood chastised as he undid the seat belt on MJ's car seat and picked the talkative little boy out of it. "Don't ever say that again, okay? Any time you see somebody get shot, you say you didn't see nothin'."

Crunchy tuned out the father and son conversation and unzipped the backpack. He closed his hand around the handle of the AR pistol and lifted it out of the bag. He detached the drum and peered in at all the .223-caliber rifle shells. There were two boxes of extra ammunition at the bottom of the backpack.

"How many bullets in this drum? Is it the whole one twenty?" Crunchy asked.

"Yeah, that whole drum full, bro," Kenwood said, taking his son in his arms and pushing open the door. "I got hellie straps for sale in case you need another one. Just have Taya hit me if you need some. Stay up, bro."

Kenwood got out, pushed the door shut, and went to his truck. He must have had his own car seat for MJ because he opened the rear passenger side door of his SUV and spent a moment getting MJ situated before shutting the door and walking around to get in the driver's seat.

Crunchy kept the backpack open between his shoes as Kenwood pulled off in the Lexus. Then, he looked through the large square windows of Mariah's Salon, and even though Nataya was looking right out at her car, he climbed over into the driver's seat and started the engine. He glanced into the salon again and smirked at the sight of Nataya jumping out of her chair, and then, he sped off down Chicago Avenue, steering with his left hand while using his right hand to dig around in her purse.

"Sorry to do you like this, Nataya," he said with a chuckle that showed he wasn't sorry at all. "It's crackin' out here, shorty. I need this car way more than you do."

Chapter 37

Nya awoke to the familiar sound of Lacey's laughter. It confused her because she'd watched Lacey leave the hotel with Marcus, Beto, and Mozzy at checkout time.

So, what was Lacey doing here at Grizzy's place?

Nya picked up her phone and slipped out of bed. She went through her suitcase and found everything she'd need for a shower. She tip-toed to the bathroom across the hall, locked the door behind her, and opened the window to let in some fresh air before she sat down on the toilet and emptied her bowels and bladder. Then, she raced into the glass doored shower stall, soaped herself up with a washcloth and Dove soap, and cleaned herself the way her mother had taught her years ago, scrubbing her skin and fingering soapy holes and then rinsing off and doing it all over again.

In the midst of showering, she thought of her father and his physical condition, only this time she managed to keep her emotions in check. She shed a couple of tears, but then, she sucked it up and set her sights on the person she knew could have very easily squashed the entire issue with Cold Gang.

His name was Stephen "Sleet" Ingram. Nya knew him well. He was a short, fat man in his early forties who lived in a white framed house on Ferdinand Street, down by Lockwood Avenue, and he'd been trying to get with Nya for years, since she was in her early teens. He'd bought her a pair of Jordans when she turned fourteen, a Louis Vuitton bag when she turned fifteen, and a bouquet of roses and a Chanel bag when she turned sixteen. On her seventeenth and eighteenth birthdays, he'd given her cash, $250 and $500 respectively.

Nya's ex-boyfriend, Deshawn, had gotten upset about the gifts. He'd called them creepy, and he'd confronted Sleet about it. Not face-to-face but privately through Facebook Messenger. And the next week, Deshawn had been chased and shot in the back as he was walking home from work.

He'd left Sleet alone after that.

In retrospect, Nya believed it may have been Deshawn's response to that incident that had ultimately led to the unravelling of their relationship. She'd lost faith in his ability to protect her. She'd always taken a liking to men who made her feel safe. After the shooting, she'd bought Deshawn a gun. She'd given him Sleet's address. And she'd waited. And waited. And waited. And when it became clear that he wasn't going to do anything, she'd broken up with him and moved on to the next ex-boyfriend, Travion Williams, the Traveling Vice Lord from the North Lauderdale neighborhood, who'd cheated on her with multiple swamp monsters. Since then, she'd said fuck a boyfriend.

Well, until now. Now, she was falling for a complete stranger she'd witnessed murder three violent gang members in cold blood, and she wasn't ashamed to admit it. Not even a little bit. All her exes had listened to gangsta music, hung out with gang members, and swore they were gangsters themselves, but none of them were like Grizzy.

Lejon "Grizzy" White was the real McCoy.

Nya had been in the shower for about fifteen minutes and was washing her hair when someone knocked at the bathroom door.

"Yeah?"

"You okay in there?" It was Lacey.

"Yeah, I'm good. I'll be out in a minute. What the heck you doing over here anyway? I thought you left the hotel with Marcus n'em?"

"I did. He came back and picked me up like two hours later. Used you as an excuse. Talkin' about I needed to get over here to be with you."

Nya heard a subtle creaking sound and figured it was Lacey leaning against the door, making herself comfortable. She'd done it hundreds of times before when Nya was in the bathroom with the door locked at their place.

"I just got off the phone with Goldie's ol' irritatin' ass wife. She said your daddy is out of surgery. He ain't woke up yet, but he should be okay. He got shot six times. You know that trauma unit is still on Covid time. Only one visitor. His wife would have to leave in order for them to let you in, and you know that clingy hoe ain't leavin' his side."

Nya turned her back to the shower heads (there were three of them) and tilted her head back to rinse out the conditioner while she ruminated over all that Lacey had just told her. She wished there was something she could do for her father, something that would put a smile on his face whenever he woke up.

"Did she say anything else?"

"Not really," Lacey answered. "Just that she has his phone and that the last call he made before he got shot was Sleet's fat ass."

Nya froze, and her teeth came together like vice grips. She stood staring through the fogged glass of the sliding shower door to the wooden door beyond it. *That fat sonofabitch*, she thought, grinding her teeth.

It was then that she came up with the perfect way to put a glorious smile on her daddy's face when he awakened from his drug-induced slumber. He'd awaken to learn that Sleet, the man responsible for his shooting, was just as dead as the gangsters who had been gunned down yesterday.

Either Nya Mixon was going to kill Sleet or she was going to die trying.

Chapter 38

Johnna Broward spent $8.1 million of her newfound wealth within three hours of getting out of bed.

Half a million was blown on a triple-white Rolls Royce Phantom for her new head of security, who'd flown home to be with his wife and kid last night and was already on his way back to Chicago. $250,000 was the amount Johnna paid her old friend, Alaina, to be her new assistant for the next year. $2 million was donated to the Victims of Violent Crime Association, and an additional $1.4 million was donated to Alexus Costilla's Feed the Nation Foundation. And the largest donation — 3.2 million — went to a secret fund Johnna had established to support the close and distant relatives of federal appeals court judge Morton Goldman, whose sole dissent would be enough to overturn her brother's conviction when he went to court in July.

The last $750,000 had been lost to random expenses — a diamond Rolex watch (also for Jayvon), a few items of high-end designer clothing Johnna had purchased online, jet fuel for her Gulfstream 650, a glam squad of beauticians to follow her around Chicago for the next couple of weeks, and a brand new $490,000 Mercedes Sprinter van that came with a shower and numerous other amenities.

She'd decided to keep the ten-man team of Secure Force bodyguards for another day. She usually only used two of them, but there were about thirty members of the paparazzi posted up outside of her Streeterville condo, all of them eager to get something out of her.

By noon, Johnna's glam squad — celebrity hairstylist and makeup artist Maria Porter and a gay male manicurist named Strangé from one of Mariah's salons — had her looking like royalty. Strangé had selected a Burberry jumpsuit with matching everything from Johnna's walk-in closet, and Johnna thought it was the perfect outfit for a rising young billionaire. Alaina directed the Secure Force driver to head for the Bostic and Staples law firm, which was just 1.8 miles away from Johnna's condo, and two brawny bodyguards helped the four of them — Johnna, Alaina, Mariah, and Strange' — climb into the back of the Sprinter seconds before it whisked them away.

"I'll be needing you all to sign non-disclosure agreements later on," Johnna said as they got comfortable on the rich, black, leather seats. She reached to Alaina for a cold bottle of Fiji water, drank from it, and handed it back. "And please, whatever you do, don't ask me anything about the shooting. We can talk about anything but that. It's still too fresh. And I have a call to make right now so try to keep it down a little."

There were head nods all around. Johnna was already putting in her AirPods and dialing Jayvon's phone number. A tiny smile raised the corners of her mouth when he answered, a smile that would have been a lot wider if not for the stitches.

"Hey, Ms. Broward," Jayvon said. "I'm en route now. Should be landing in the next twenty minutes or so. How you feeling this morning?"

"A lot better than yesterday," Johnna replied, reclining her seat. "Have you seen the news?"

"Of *course* I've seen it. *Congratulations*! I know it's a sad time for Panteon, but I'm glad you were able to get something good out of this whole mess."

"Yeah," she said dreamily as Alaina pressed play on a soothing R&B hit from Beyoncé's Renaissance album.

"I was able to get you."

Jayvon paused. Then, "That's not what I meant." He chuckled nervously. "I was talking about the reported rise in your net worth from Panteon's stock gains. I saw it on Good Morning America. But yeah, I suppose what we have is kind of special too, huh?"

Johnna's expression tightened. She didn't like that uncomfortable pause nor did she like that he considered their entanglement as only 'kind of' special.

"What'd you say to your wife?" Johnna asked, studying her flawless new manicure.

"I haven't told her anything yet. Can't lie though, I've been ready to leave her for a while. All we do is argue. She wants more from me than I can give, and I'm way past tired of it. I was about ready to call it quits for good when she got pregnant with our kid. That's the only reason I stuck it out for this long."

A glimmer of hope brightened Johnna's disposition. "Listen," she said as Marian began touching up her eye shadow, "I bought you a Rolls Royce a few hours ago. It'll be delivered to my mansion in The Hamptons tomorrow morning, so you'll have that to drive whenever we're in the New York area. I ordered you an iced-out Rolex that'll be shipped here to Chicago overnight from Zo Frost. I'll get you a new wardrobe and whatever else you need, and I'll get you the very best divorce attorney money can buy. I'll pay off your wife, so we can get full custody of your daughter, if that's what you want. I just want you here with me from now on. I need you right now."

Alaina and the glam squad froze and looked at Johnna. Strangé, a slender, light-skinned man with a colorful fade and face full of makeup, brought one hand up to cover his mouth.

Jayvon didn't hesitate. "I want you too, Johnna. I've always wanted you. I mean, I know a lot of men are attracted to you because of your success but forget all that. You are an amazingly beautiful woman. You understand that? A beauty, a boss, and an inspiration to so many other Black women out there." He took a moment to laugh. "And shit, you just bought me a fuckin' Rolls Royce! Yo! That's *mad* crazy."

"So, is that a yes?" Johnna asked, her smile so wide now that it hurt a little.

"Hell yes it's a yes!" He laughed again. "Where do I sign?"

It was Johnna's turn to laugh. It was as if a bubble of happiness had exploded inside the Sprinter van as it pulled up to the eighty-six story MTN Tower on Wabash Avenue. Maria and Alaina were all smiles, and Strangé was slapping his armrest with excitement.

"Great," Johnna said, beaming. "I have an appointment with my attorney. There's an armored Mercedes waiting for you at the airport. The driver will give you a black credit card and take you straight to the Magnificent Mile. It's kind of life Fifth Avenue in New York. All the designer stores are right there. Spend as much as you'd like but hurry up. I want you naked and in bed when I walk back through that door."

Jayvon's contagious laughter filled her ears again, and Johnna ended the call with a huge smile on her face. She looked at the smiling faces all around her and said, "What?"

"Okay, so can we talk about this?" Strangé asked, obviously thirsty to know who it was Johnna had been on the phone with. "Or can we at least see who he is? 'Cause I *know* he gotta be fine as hell if you trickin' like *that*."

Johnna rolled her eyes. She went to a TikTok video from Jayvon's days as a personal trainer and showed it to her three nosey companions as a bodyguard pulled open the Sprinter's sliding side door.

"Mmm hmm." Alaina nodded approvingly. She and Mariah nodded their heads in unison. Jayvon was all pecs and abs in the video as he put his exercise on hold to take a swallow of vitamin water and flex in front of the mirror.

Strangé slipped down out of his seat, as if he'd fainted, and everyone laughed merrily as they stepped out of the van and allowed five burly Secure Force bodyguards to escort them into the MTN Tower, where not only MTN News was produced but also where the Bostic and Staples law firm was located.

Johnna Broward had no idea that, within the next couple of minutes, her joyful smile would be turned upside down.

Chapter 39

"Are you sure you wanna do this?"

"One hundred percent." Nya pulled the black ski mask down over her face, slid the thirty-shot clip into her 9-millimeter Glock pistol, and snatched back the slide, chambering a round. "And I want Crunchy and Wobble after this."

She and Grizzy were in the Trackhawk. Lacey and Marcus were two car lengths behind them in Marcus's slime green Dodge Charger Hellcat. They were on Ferdinand Street, parked just across the street from Sleet's house. They'd been sitting there for over twenty minutes now, Nya staring out her tinted window at the house across the street, Grizzy holding his Draco with his ski mask rolled up to his forehead, Future's *I Never Liked You* album playing at low volume from the Trackhawk's Bose speaker system.

There weren't many people on the street. Two preteen boys on bikes were leaning against a chain linked fence two houses down from Sleet's place, interacting with the four young girls who were jumping rope on the sidewalk. An older woman, who might have been in her late sixties or early seventies, was sitting on a porch at the far end of the block, talking on a smartphone and holding an electronic portable fan up to her leathery old face. That was it.

Sleet's black Range Rover was parked at the curb in front of his house. The front door to the house had opened eight minutes ago, but it had closed a second later, frustrating Nya.

She was overly emotional now. She'd received a frantic call from her stepmother, saying her father had gone into cardiac arrest and had been rushed back into the room they'd taken him to for his surgical procedures. Nya hadn't heard anything since then, and she likely wouldn't since they'd all left their phones at Grizzy's place out south.

"You know I'll do this shit for you, right?" Grizzy said.

Nya ignored him. She kept her eyes on Sleet's front door and the large picture window at the forefront of his living room. The curtains were closed. She knew Sleet was in there somewhere, and she wondered who else was in there with him. She knew he was engaged to a girl she'd gone to school with, but she couldn't remember the girl's name.

"Nya. Talk to me." Grizzy reached over and tugged on the sleeve of her snug, black hoodie. "Lift up that mask and look at me."

She sighed and followed orders, lifting the mask and turning to look at him. She wished she could stop her eyes from watering, but she couldn't. Images of her hospitalized father kept flickering across her mind. Goldie lying on a gurney, surrounded by doctors and nurses and blinding white lights.

"What the fuck do you want, Lejon?"

Grizzy grinned his sexy grin, took Nya's chin in his hand, and leaned in to kiss her on the lips. He thumbed away her tears and kissed her again. "We got this," he said. "And once we nail this nigga, I'm taking you out on a real date. For your birthday. Our first official date. Then, we're going to the Bahamas for a week. Just me and you. A'ight?"

Nya sniffled. Nodded. "Me and Lacey had plans to celebrate my birthday at Redbone's tonight. It's a strip club on 16th Street. Lotto and Cardi B are supposed to be performing. Shit gon' be too lit." She turned back to look out her window. She sighed again, pondered over her situation with Grizzy, and said, "Is this, like, some one-night stand type shit? 'Cause if it is, you can tell me. I can take it."

"That ain't what I want it to be," Grizzy answered without a moment's hesitation. "I been single for a while. Been lookin' for a woman like you, somebody I can have fun with but who also knows how to be a smart, gangsta bitch at the same time. You showed me from the start that you had some gangsta in you. And I *know* I can trust you. I feel it in my chest. That's some once in a blue type shit, and I ain't gon' take it for granted."

Another small nod from Nya, this one accompanied by a tender little smirk. She felt the same way about Grizzy. She'd been single ever since Travion because she wanted a real nigga who would dick her down in private and protect her in public, a man she wouldn't have to be beefing with bitches on social media over because he couldn't keep his dick in his pants when she wasn't around. Money was a plus, but it wasn't necessarily a requirement. She could help a nigga get some money. It was that intelligent street mentality she was looking for — that and some really good dick — and Grizzy checked all the boxes.

She lowered her gaze to the pistol on her lap. Her mind found traction on the idea of vacationing in the Bahamas with Grizzy, and it made her think of Butch and his family's vacation in Brazil. She'd checked Instagram after her shower and watched the video of them boarding a private jet on his daughter, Lauren's page, so she knew there was at least some truth to Butch's story.

"What's your next move with Butch?" Nya asked, looking over at Grizzy again. "You know he ain't got the cash now. You want me and Lacey to just try and finesse him out of as much as we can?"

He shook his head, leaning forward and looking past her, his attention at Sleet's front door.

"Nah," he said. "Fuck that rat ass nigga. Whatever Lacey wanna do is on her, but I don't want you going back around him. I texted my old man about it. Ain't no way to get that much money outta somebody's bank account without catchin' a case. I'd have a better chance going at Johnna herself. She prob'ly don't even remember me. My lil sister used to hang out with her in the Gardens when they were kids, but I don't think she done heard from Johnna in years."

"That $30 million wasn't all of your daddy's money, was it?"

"Nope. Over the past few years, he done bought me and my mama all kinds of shit. He bought that house I live in and all my cars too. Paid cash for all of it. He paid over six hundred thousand for a house in Atlanta, so my mama could have a second spot down there. He paid off my lil sister's house in Country Club Hills and bought her two new cars. Don't ask me where he got all that money from, 'cause he been gone for almost twenty years, but he just started blowin' money fast a couple years ago."

"Hmm." Nya turned to look at Sleet's front door again… just as it swung open.

Sleet's fiancée walked out first, holding the hand of a toddler who couldn't have been older than three. Nya remembered the girl's name now. It was Valencia Ford. She'd sat next to Nya in geometry class. She was a tall, pretty, mulatto girl with long, curly hair and a quiet disposition, and the little boy, whose hand she was holding, had her same high yellow complexion.

Sleet came out behind them, pulling the door shut and locking it. He was smiling, talking to Valencia, wearing a white Gucci shirt with matching shorts and shoes. His fat, round belly made the shirt rise up in the front. He had a black handgun on his lap, right under the left side of his belly.

"Run up on him real fast," Grizzy said. "Just breathe, get up close on him, and do your thing. I'll be right there behind you."

Nya hesitated. Her eyes were glued to Sleet and seeing him all happy and healthy while her father was all fucked up in the hospital made her blood boil, but she still couldn't bring herself to open her door.

And then, a pearl white Chevy Tahoe came riding past, and Sleet yelled to one of its passengers. "Ay, you hear what happened to that nigga, Goldie, last night? Heard they hit that nigga like seven, eight times." He laughed, slapping the banister as he started down the stairs behind his lady and son.

Nya pulled down her mask, threw open her door, and hopped out. A blast of adrenaline surged through her as her black Nike Air Max sneakers hit the ground. She came from around the front of the Trackhawk with her gun raised in both hands, like her father had taught her at the shooting range when she was fourteen. She completely ignored the white Tahoe that was rolling past.

Like a lovestruck protagonist in a cheesy romance novel, she only had eyes for Sleet. Sleet was about 5'5" while Nya was only 4'10". Valencia and her boy were already out of the yard and walking toward the Range Rover, and Sleet was just swinging one foot off the last porch step.

His eyes got big. He reached for the gun under his massive gut, and Nya, aiming and running, opened fire.

Phop. Phop. Phop. Phop. Phop. Phop.

She heard frightened screams from Valencia and the kids down the block, and she saw Sleet's head jerk back as one round tore through the side of his neck. Two more of the six shots hit him high in the chest, but he still managed to get his gun loose from his waistline and raise it in one flimsy hand.

Nya was fearless. She had stopped on the sidewalk, and even as she looked down the barrel of his gun and saw the flames plume from inside it, she was squeezing the trigger again. *Phop. Phop. Phop. Phop. Phop. Phop.* Each round found its mark with two of them piercing perfectly round holes in Sleet's wide, brown forehead and the others tearing through his jaw and chin and the center of his chest as he went down, falling backward onto the porch steps.

More gunfire erupted from somewhere behind Nya, but she paid it only a glance. It was Marcus, Lacey, and Grizzy, firing on the white Tahoe and a man who had jumped out of its passenger door with a gun aimed at Nya. She ran into the yard and stood over Sleet. He was clearly already dead, the multiple holes in his face round and bleeding, but Nya aimed at his brow and shot him eight more times.

When she turned to run back to the Trackhawk, she was surprised to find Lacey and Marcus standing side by side in the middle of the street, firing their guns at the fleeing Tahoe, while Grizzy stood over the man who'd jumped out of the Tahoe and pumped him full of bullets. The teenage girls, who'd been jumping rope, and the two boys, who'd been sitting on their bikes, were all face down on the sidewalk with the palms of their hands pressed against their ears. Valencia was squatting down next to the Range Rover, hugging her son tight against her chest with her head down, crying as the thunderous gunfire continued.

Nya hurried back to the passenger's side of the Trackhawk. She pulled open her door and got in, and Grizzy climbed in beside her.

The Trackhawk took off like a rocket, trailed closely by Marcus's Hellcat.

Nya snatched off her ski mask and threw it to the floor with her gun. She dropped her visor mirror and ran her fingers through her frazzled hair. Grizzy pushed his mask to the top of his head and used his teeth to pull off his leather, black gloves.

"My heart is beating so fast right now," Nya said shakily. She pushed the visor up and leaned back in her seat, checking the sideview mirror as Grizzy and Marcus made one turn after another.

"Where to now?" Grizzy asked breathlessly. "You said some'n about Crunchy and Wobble. Where they at?"

Nya hesitated but only for a moment. She took a few seconds to breathe and settle her nerves. Then, she sat forward and gave Grizzy directions to the blighted section of Leamington Avenue where the Wicket Town faction of Traveling Vice Lords was located.

Grizzy didn't say another word. He just drove.

Chapter 40

Nikkia Staples possessed the kind of exceptional beauty that didn't require a layer of cosmetics in order for her to turn heads when she walked into a room, but she'd put on some anyway, along with a black, leather, Valentino skirt and a dark gray, designer blouse. She stood and stepped around her desk to shake Johnna's hand as Johnna and Alaina walked into her huge corner office, the floor-to-ceiling windows behind her reminding Johnna of the views from her Streeterville condo.

Smiling, Johnna looked from Nikkia to Alana. The two women were the same light brown complexion, equally pretty, and were dressed quite similarly, only Alaina was still carrying the excess weight she'd gained during pregnancy, and her blouse was black, though a lighter shade of black than her skirt.

"Afternoon, ladies," Nikkia said as she returned to her swivel chair behind the desk.

"This is my assistant, Alaina," Johnna said and took a seat in one of the two white, leather armchairs in front of the large, glass top desk.

Alaina sat down in the other seat, and they looked at Nikkia as the wealthy, young, celebrity attorney interlaced her fingers on the desk and stared blankly at Johnna.

"You sure you want your assistant to hear this?" Nikkia asked.

"Sure." Johnna sat back a little, her brow knitted, and placed her phone face down on her lap. "Why do you look so down? I'm the one who almost lost my life yesterday. You'd think it happened to you."

There was an uncomfortable silence. Nikkia's indecipherable expression remained intact. A bald eagle soared past outside the window behind her, its wings fully extended, the long, brown feathers fluttering in the breeze.

"Has she signed an NDA yet?" Nikkia asked finally.

"No, not yet. I told her she'd need to though." Johnna glanced over at Alaina, whose round, brown face looked almost stunned beneath the curly, brown wig on her head.

"I won't say anything. I swear," said Alaina.

Another pause from Nikkia. Then, she took in a deep breath and let it all out.

"The Lower Manhattan district attorney just sent me a notice saying they'll be going to a grand jury sometime within the next hour or so to file criminal charges against you for felony assault. They have video of you attacking one of your employees shortly before the shooting took place. A woman named Diana Martin-Caldwell. She's already filed a police report, and she's pressing charges. I'm being told that she's married to Michael Caldwell and that your assaulting her may have set him off."

Johnna's gloss coated lips fell apart. Her thoughts shattered into a thousand pieces, like a completed one-thousand-piece jigsaw puzzle thrown against a wall. But if there was one quality that Johnna had acquired on her road to riches, it was resilience. She began to put the many pieces of thought back together as hastily as possible.

"Okay," she said, getting up from the chair and starting to pace. "Tiffany Stingley was with Diana when the fight went down. Tip won't make any statements against me, but I'll pay her to fabricate something that'll make me look good in the public's eyes."

"What happened?" Nikkia asked. "What were you fighting over?"

"She walked past me with Tip, and I thought I heard her mumble something under her breath. I asked her what she'd said, and she snapped at me. Said, 'You heard me! He didn't fucking deserve to be fired!' And I whooped that fat hoe right then and there."

Alaina choked on a laugh and received a tight eyed look from Nikkia for the transgression.

"What's Tiffany Stingley's phone number?" Nikkia asked, picking up her iPhone. Johnna went to her list of contacts and read off the number, and Nikkia saved it to her phone. "Okay, text her and let her know I'll be calling her shortly. Right now, you and I have more important things to discuss."

"More important than being charged with a felony?" Johnna asked snappishly.

Nikkia stared silently at Johnna's frustrated scowl. "I've already contacted Jamia Lloyd's mother and offered her your condolences," she said after a moment. "She agreed to accept $15 million, and she'll sign an agreement promising not to sue. I asked Anthony Ferguson's husband if $10 million would be enough to compensate him for his loss, and he said you've done so much for him and Anthony that he wouldn't even think of suing. I still recommend sending him $10 million before people start getting in his ear. Romero Alvarez's wife and parents are all in the country illegally, so I don't see them trying to sue. Still may be good to compensate them as well though. We'll have to fight with Tabby Green's family attorney. He's asking for $100 million, and he's threatening a trial if the money's not paid in full within the next thirty days."

"Go on and pay them all," Johnna said, essentially waving off the settlement payments. She went to her Chase banking app and wired $135 million to Nikkia's checking account without a second thought, and she went back to pacing worriedly over the pending criminal charges she was facing. "Does this mean I'll be arrested?"

"For the cameras, basically. Won't be all that different from how they treated Trump. You'll be in and out of there in a matter of minutes, and you'll never do any time. The felony charge'll be dropped to a misdemeanor, and the court will order you to attend some anger management classes. They're doing this more for shock value than anything. It'll be all over the news. They'll feel like they have somebody to blame for the Panteon shooting. Which is why I want to get those settlements paid out and those NDAs signed before you turn yourself in, so those families can't come out and start saying they feel like you're responsible for all this."

Johnna stopped pacing and stood with her fists at the waist of her Burberry jumpsuit, licking at the stitches in her lip and thinking. *Shit! What the fuck have I done?*

And the scandal wasn't over. She still had Butch to deal with. Pandy was managing that whole situation, and she trusted Pandy like she trusted Alaina, but when Butch returned from Rio in a couple of weeks, only to be gunned down a short time later, there was a very real chance that his murder could come back and bite her on the ass just like her fight with Diana had. She knew she could easily just pay him off, but she didn't feel like that was the right thing to do. Butch was the federal informant who'd gotten the White Moes indicted from the start. She'd rather die than to pay him that $22 million.

"What are you thinking?" Nikkia asked, folding her arms across her chest and leaning back in her chair.

"What I'm thinking?" Johnna stared vacantly at her high-priced attorney, the smile she'd worn walking into the office a distant memory. "I think it might be best to keep that to myself."

Chapter 41

"The side of your neck is bleeding."

"No, it ain't."

"It is. Fuck would I lie about that for?" Grizzy reached over and touched his thumb to the side of Nya's neck then showed her the blood on the pink skin of his inner thumb. "See?"

He watched, mesmerized by her incomparable beauty, as she frantically yanked down the visor and tilted her head to the right to expose the left side of her neck to the mirror. It was clear to him what had happened. A bullet from Sleet's gun had skated across the side of her neck. A minor graze wound.

"I'm shot?!" Nya said, all high-pitched and panicky.

Grizzy chuckled at the urgency in her tone. "You're good, lil mama. It ain't shit but a graze wound. I'll go in there and get you some napkins. See if they got some Band-Aids. Keep your eyes open."

They were at the Marathon gas station on Madison and Leamington Avenue, in what Nya had described as an undisputed Wicked Town territory. Grizzy and Marcus had parked side by side in front of the building with the front ends of their vehicles facing outward, so they could keep watch on the entire intersection and also make a quick getaway if things went left.

Grizzy looked around one last time before deciding it was safe to get out. There was a squad of loud talking, young niggas walking past on Leamington and a red Monte Carlo full of them at one gas pump, all of their hats cocked to the hard left, but Grizzy didn't feel threatened. He had a Glock with a switch under his black Gucci tee shirt (which, he'd realized, was the exact same shirt Sleet had been wearing, just a different color), and Nya had her Glock on her lap. Plus, he had Marcus with him and Lacey, who had proved to be just as gangster as her much shorter friend. If an altercation were to arise, Grizzy knew for certain that his group would open fire without question.

He pushed open his door and stepped down from his Jeep Grand Cherokee Trackhawk. He shouted for Marcus, who instantly rose from the driver's seat of his slime green Dodge Charger Hellcat and accompanied Grizzy into the gas station.

As they walked through the door, Grizzy glanced back at the Monte Carlo and saw that one of the boys was watching them. So were the three grown women who walked in behind them, only their stares were more sexual in nature.

"Mm mm *mmm*," one woman hummed lustfully. "Where y'all come from? I ain't never seen you or him."

Grizzy regarded her with a warm smile. She was about 5'8" and thick in all the right places. Her hair and nails were done to perfection, and her plain white tee shirt and white denim jeans were skintight, revealing her every curve. She was a bad ass redbone who reminded Grizzy of Ari Fletcher, Moneybagg Yo's current girlfriend. Her two friends were dressed in similar fashion, though they weren't nearly as appealing.

"Folks," Marcus said, taking Grizzy's attention away from the woman. "Grab some blunts and a pack of squares. I'll grab us a few crème sodas and some cups. I still got a pint of Wock in the car. I gotta pour me up a four after that shit that just went down."

"Man, that shit was crazy." Grizzy went to the counter and had the clerk take down one pack of Newport's and three

STEPPERS | KING RIO

packs of cigarillos. He intended on smoking an entire ounce of exotic bud once they made it back to his place out south.

He also intended on fucking the everlasting shit out of Nya Mixon as soon as they walked through the door. He'd never felt so attracted to a woman in all his life, and he knew it had everything to do with him seeing her hop out of his truck and run down on Sleet before the short whale of a man could even make it off the porch steps. He'd caught a fleeting glimpse of her standing over Sleet and shooting him multiple times in the head. It had all happened in a flash, while Grizzy was busy shooting the dreadlocks off the guy who'd tried to come to Sleet's rescue, but it was a memory he knew he'd never forget.

He pulled out a bankroll and was thumbing through the hundreds and fifties, searching for the twenties, when he glanced outside and saw a small, gray Ford Focus pull onto the gas station platform. The windows weren't tinted, and even from a distance, Grizzy was immediately able to recognize the driver as Crunchy.

Grizzy watched Crunchy get out of the car. Two of the boys, who'd been walking past on Leamington, changed course and headed toward Crunchy, yelling to him in a way that told Grizzy they were his friends. Two of the boys from the Monte Carlo got out and shook hands with Crunchy. A gang handshake. Two Ts and a drop of the "rakes," the latter a sign of disrespect to Gangster Disciples like Grizzy and Marcus.

Clenching his teeth, Grizzy paid for the blunts and cigarettes and took the plastic bag the clerk put them in. One of the women, who'd walked in behind him, looked outside and said, "Shit, girl, that's Crunchy. I gotta ask him about Curry."

Grizzy's eyes flicked over to his Trackhawk and Marcus's Hellcat. He was glad to see that Nya and Lacey hadn't gotten out to confront Crunchy.

Not yet at least.

Much to Grizzy's relief, Crunchy did the same handshake with the other boys, spoke with them for a couple of seconds, and climbed right back into the Focus. When the corpulent young woman, who wanted to know about Curry, went out and stood next to the Focus, blocking Crunchy's view into the gas station, Grizzy walked out the door and slipped back into his Trackhawk.

"That's Crunchy right there," Nya said before Grizzy could even pull his door shut. "In that Ford Focus."

"That's definitely him," said Lacey. She had lowered the driver's window in the Hellcat and was holding Marcus's mini Draco in both hands.

"We can't do shit right here," Nya said. "Not with all these cameras."

Marcus came walking out of the gas station seconds later, and the boy, who'd watched Grizzy and Marcus enter the building, had his eyes on Marcus as he exited the building. The boy said something to another boy in the Monte Carlo. Then, everyone turned to look at Marcus as he headed toward his Charger. The Monte Carlo's doors swung open just as Crunchy began cruising away in the Focus.

There was a sudden blur in Grizzy's periphery, and when he looked over at Nya, he saw that she had snatched his Draco from between his center console. As he pulled the Glock from inside his black, Amiri jeans, Nya lifted herself out of the passenger window and sat on the ledge with the Draco aimed at the two young dreadheads who'd just emerged from the Monte Carlo with their hands under their shirts.

"Y'all don't wanna do that," Nya warned, and the boys froze in their tracks as Grizzy started the engine and lowered the window. He aimed his Glock with one hand and steered with the other, his eyes flicking from the two potential jackers to the Ford Focus he was following onto Leamington Avenue. Nya slipped back down into the truck, still holding the Draco on the boys at the gas station as she left them standing on the platform with stunned expressions on their brown, young faces. Grizzy checked his rearview mirror and saw that the slime green Charger was trailing close behind him.

Heart pounding, Grizzy stepped down on the gas, his eyes glued to the Ford Focus in front of him. They were just approaching the corner of Monroe and Leamington when he veered around to the driver's side of the Focus and stomped down on the brake pedal.

Nya didn't bother putting on her ski-mask. She threw open her door, hopped out, and got so close up on the small, gray car that the short barrel of the Draco pistol tapped against the closed glass of Crunchy's window, and when he looked over at her, his eyes widening in surprise and fear, she pulled the trigger.

The glass shattered, and Crunchy's head was thrown violently to the side as several 7.62-millimeter rounds slammed through his skull.

Epilogue
Abaco Island, the Bahamas

"How you doin', Daddy?"

"I'm a'ight, baby girl. I'm alive. That's all that matters, ain't it?"

"Yep. You're alive, and that punk ass nigga, Sleet, is dead as a doorknob."

"Yeah, I read about that. Some niggas caught him comin' out his house over there on Ferdinand. His nephew got killed too, right in the middle of the street. I'm glad. That nigga snaked me. Told me everything was good then clicked over and told some lil niggas to hit me up. If it wasn't for Lil Head being in that gas station and overhearing it, I wouldn't be here today."

"Awww. Tell my uncle, Lil Head, to call me. Not this weekend though. I got company this weekend."

"It's that GD nigga, ain't it?"

Nya laughed and nodded her head vehemently. Grizzy watched her do it. The two of them were reclined in lounge chairs on the balcony of their twenty-second floor, rented condominium at the Bahama Beach Club on Abaco Island in the Bahamas. Nya wore a Brown Girl Grinding tee shirt over the white, two-piece, Fendi bikini Grizzy had bought her from a designer shopping boutique when they landed at the Nassau airport. Grizzy wore nothing but a white pair of Balenciaga swimming trunks.

He looked at his own iPhone while Nya spoke with her father on FaceTime. The Shade Room had just shared the mugshot from Johnna Broward's arrest for assaulting the wife of the man who'd gone human hunting inside Panteon Tech three days ago. Which was no surprise to Grizzy; his younger sister, Alaina, was now Johnna Broward's personal assistant, and she'd already told him all about the felony arrest warrant before it was even announced. According to Black Twitter, the government was only trying to sabotage Johnna's company by charging her for the so-called "petty dispute" between her and one of her employees, and as a result, the Black community had come together to buy even more Panteon stocks and products.

Johnna Broward's net worth had reportedly risen to $11.3 billion.

Grizzy put his phone down and turned his head to look at Nya as she said goodbye to her old man and ended the FaceTime call. Her whole face was one big smile. She drank from her fruity alcoholic beverage and then placed it and her phone on the table between them. She got up from her lounge chair and mounted Grizzy on his.

"You wanna go back down to the pool?" Nya asked, lowering her head to plant a kiss on his naked chest. Her small, delicate hands rubbed and kneaded his pectoral muscles, his shoulders, his abs. "Or do you wanna head back inside?"

Grizzy answered by getting to his feet, supporting Nya's full weight in the one hand he held under her ass, and stepping into his Amiri flip-flops. He French kissed her as he carried her through the patio door, across the smooth, hardwood floor of the living room, and up the wide hallway to their master bedroom suite.

Nya lost the Brown Girl Grinding shirt before they had even crossed the threshold. Her top went next, and when Grizzy threw her onto the bed, she laughed as she removed the bikini bottom and tossed it aside.

Grizzy fell on top of her, kissing on her succulent lips, nibbling at her cute, little chin, sucking on the side of her neck that had suffered a graze wound just two days ago. She put her hands on the top of his head and shoved his face down toward the lips she *really* wanted him to kiss, so he kissed and licked and sucked her there, holding the backs of her ankles in his strong, dark hands and pushing her legs way up by her head.

The sweet scent of her pussy made him salivate with hunger. He parted her thick vaginal lips and ran the flat of his tongue between them, savoring the escaping juices while he used his thumb to massage her rigid clitoris.

"Okay, okay, okay," Nya said quickly. She reached down and lifted his chin, so he could look at her. "Fuck all that. I want that dick. I want you to fuck the shit outa me *right… now.*"

"We're all out of condoms, baby."

Nya pouted. She seemed to be genuinely saddened by the news. Then, she pulled him up, kissed him on the mouth, and reached down into his shorts to pull out his rock-hard erection. She rubbed the head between her soft, wet pussy lips and then eased it in. Her mouth fell open, and she sucked in a breath as Grizzy used his weight to dive in deep.

They went at it for a long while, and in three different positions, from missionary to doggy and finally to reverse cowgirl, which was how their energetic fuck session ended, with Nya riding him until his semen was oozing down the length of his dick.

Afterwards, Nya collapsed on top of him, smiling and panting and laughing a little. When their breathing settled a bit, she rested her chin on his chest and looked up into his eyes.

"Shit," she said. "Yes. If I get pregnant from this, it was worth it. You can fuck me like that every single day for the rest of my life."

Grizzy chuckled at the thought of her becoming pregnant. He squeezed her impossibly soft ass cheeks in his hands and stared longingly into her pretty, light brown eyes. Looking at her now, he found it difficult to think of her as the same gangsta bitch who'd murdered two men in cold blood just two days ago.

The vivid memory of her standing over Sleet appeared in Grizzy's mind. Her aiming the Glock at Sleet's face. Fire spitting repeatedly from the gun barrel. Sleet's head jerking back against the porch step from the impact of every round fired. Nya Mixon was a stunningly attractive, young woman, but there was no question about it. Deep down, she was just as gangster as Lejon White.

Which reminded him: With his father's money in Johnna Broward's possession, there was really no need in letting Butch live any longer. Butch had snitched on Willie White and stolen $30 million of Willie White's money. Now, Grizzy was going to make Butch pay for it.

And in the famous words of Memphis rapper Pooh Shiesty, Grizzy was going to get it back in blood.

To be continued...

Lock Down Publications and Ca$h Presents
Assisted Publishing Packages

BASIC PACKAGE	UPGRADED PACKAGE
$499	$800
Editing	Typing
Cover Design	Editing
Formatting	Cover Design
	Formatting
ADVANCE PACKAGE	**LDP SUPREME PACKAGE**
$1,200	$1,500
Typing	Typing
Editing	Editing
Cover Design	Cover Design
Formatting	Formatting
Copyright registration	Copyright registration
Proofreading	Proofreading
Upload book to Amazon	Set up Amazon account
	Upload book to Amazon
	Advertise on LDP, Amazon and
	Facebook Page

***Other services available upon request.
Additional charges may apply

Lock Down Publications
P.O. Box 944
Stockbridge, GA 30281-9998
Phone: 470 303-9761

Submission Guideline

Submit the first three chapters of your completed manuscript to ldpsubmissions@gmail.com. In the subject line add **Your Book's Title**. The manuscript must be in a Word Doc file and sent as an attachment. Document should be in Times New Roman, double spaced, and in size 12 font. Also, provide your synopsis and full contact information. If sending multiple submissions, they must each be in a separate email.

Have a story but no way to send it electronically? You can still submit to LDP/Ca$h Presents. Send in the first three chapters, written or typed, of your completed manuscript to:

LDP: Submissions Dept
P.O. Box 944
Stockbridge, GA 30281-9998

DO NOT send original manuscript. Must be a duplicate.
Provide your synopsis and a cover letter containing your full contact information.

Thanks for considering LDP and Ca$h Presents.

NEW RELEASES

SANCTIFIED AND HORNY
by **XTASY**

THE PLUG OF LIL MEXICO 2
by **CHRIS GREEN**

THE BLACK DIAMOND CARTEL
by **SAYNOMORE**

THE BIRTH OF A GANGSTER 3
by **DELMONT PLAYER**

Coming Soon from Lock Down Publications/Ca$h Presents

BLOOD OF A BOSS VI
SHADOWS OF THE GAME II
TRAP BASTARD II
By **Askari**

LOYAL TO THE GAME IV
By **T.J. & Jelissa**

TRUE SAVAGE VIII
MIDNIGHT CARTEL IV
DOPE BOY MAGIC IV
CITY OF KINGZ III
NIGHTMARE ON SILENT AVE II
THE PLUG OF LIL MEXICO II
CLASSIC CITY II
By **Chris Green**

BLAST FOR ME III
A SAVAGE DOPEBOY III
CUTTHROAT MAFIA III
DUFFLE BAG CARTEL VII
HEARTLESS GOON VI
By **Ghost**

A HUSTLER'S DECEIT III
KILL ZONE II
BAE BELONGS TO ME III
TIL DEATH II
By **Aryanna**

KING OF THE TRAP III
By **T.J. Edwards**

GORILLAZ IN THE BAY V
3X KRAZY III
STRAIGHT BEAST MODE III
By **De'Kari**

KINGPIN KILLAZ IV
STREET KINGS III
PAID IN BLOOD III
CARTEL KILLAZ IV
DOPE GODS III
By **Hood Rich**

SINS OF A HUSTLA II
By **ASAD**

YAYO V
BRED IN THE GAME 2
By **S. Allen**

THE STREETS WILL TALK II
By **Yolanda Moore**

SON OF A DOPE FIEND III
HEAVEN GOT A GHETTO III
SKI MASK MONEY III
By **Renta**

LOYALTY AIN'T PROMISED III
By **Keith Williams**

I'M NOTHING WITHOUT HIS LOVE II
SINS OF A THUG II
TO THE THUG I LOVED BEFORE II
IN A HUSTLER I TRUST II
By **Monet Dragun**

QUIET MONEY IV
EXTENDED CLIP III
THUG LIFE IV
By **Trai'Quan**

THE STREETS MADE ME IV
By **Larry D. Wright**

IF YOU CROSS ME ONCE III
ANGEL V
By **Anthony Fields**

THE STREETS WILL NEVER CLOSE IV
By **K'ajji**

HARD AND RUTHLESS III
KILLA KOUNTY IV
By **Khufu**

MONEY GAME III
By **Smoove Dolla**

MURDA WAS THE CASE III
Elijah R. Freeman

AN UNFORESEEN LOVE IV
BABY, I'M WINTERTIME COLD III
By **Meesha**

QUEEN OF THE ZOO III
By **Black Migo**

CONFESSIONS OF A JACKBOY III
By **Nicholas Lock**

JACK BOYS VS DOPE BOYS IV
A GANGSTA'S QUR'AN V
COKE GIRLZ II
COKE BOYS II
LIFE OF A SAVAGE V
CHI'RAQ GANGSTAS V
SOSA GANG III
BRONX SAVAGES II
BODYMORE KINGPINS II
By **Romell Tukes**

KING KILLA II
By **Vincent "Vitto" Holloway**

BETRAYAL OF A THUG III
By **Fre$h**

THE MURDER QUEENS III
By **Michael Gallon**

THE BIRTH OF A GANGSTER III
By **Delmont Player**

TREAL LOVE II
By **Le'Monica Jackson**

FOR THE LOVE OF BLOOD III
By **Jamel Mitchell**

STEPPERS | KING RIO

RAN OFF ON DA PLUG II
By **Paper Boi Rari**

HOOD CONSIGLIERE III
By **Keese**

PRETTY GIRLS DO NASTY THINGS II
By **Nicole Goosby**

PROTÉGÉ OF A LEGEND III
LOVE IN THE TRENCHES II
By **Corey Robinson**

IT'S JUST ME AND YOU II
By **Ah'Million**

FOREVER GANGSTA III
By **Adrian Dulan**

GORILLAZ IN THE TRENCHES II
By **SayNoMore**

THE COCAINE PRINCESS VIII
By **King Rio**

CRIME BOSS II
By **Playa Ray**

LOYALTY IS EVERYTHING III
By **Molotti**

HERE TODAY GONE TOMORROW II
By **Fly Rock**

207

STEPPERS | KING RIO

REAL G'S MOVE IN SILENCE II
By **Von Diesel**

GRIMEY WAYS IV
By **Ray Vinci**

Available Now

RESTRAINING ORDER I & II
By **CA$H & Coffee**

LOVE KNOWS NO BOUNDARIES I II & III
By **Coffee**

RAISED AS A GOON I, II, III & IV
BRED BY THE SLUMS I, II, III
BLAST FOR ME I & II
ROTTEN TO THE CORE I II III
A BRONX TALE I, II, III
DUFFLE BAG CARTEL I II III IV V VI
HEARTLESS GOON I II III IV V
A SAVAGE DOPEBOY I II
DRUG LORDS I II III
CUTTHROAT MAFIA I II
KING OF THE TRENCHES
By **Ghost**

LAY IT DOWN I & II
LAST OF A DYING BREED I II
BLOOD STAINS OF A SHOTTA I & II III
By **Jamaica**

LOYAL TO THE GAME I II III
LIFE OF SIN I, II III
By **TJ & Jelissa**

IF LOVING HIM IS WRONG…I & II
LOVE ME EVEN WHEN IT HURTS I II III
By **Jelissa**

STEPPERS | KING RIO

BLOODY COMMAS I & II
SKI MASK CARTEL I, II & III
KING OF NEW YORK I II, III IV V
RISE TO POWER I II III
COKE KINGS I II III IV V
BORN HEARTLESS I II III IV
KING OF THE TRAP I II
By **T.J. Edwards**

WHEN THE STREETS CLAP BACK I & II III
THE HEART OF A SAVAGE I II III IV
MONEY MAFIA I II
LOYAL TO THE SOIL I II III
By **Jibril Williams**

A DISTINGUISHED THUG STOLE MY HEART I II &
III
LOVE SHOULDN'T HURT I II III IV
RENEGADE BOYS I II III IV
PAID IN KARMA I II III
SAVAGE STORMS I II III
AN UNFORESEEN LOVE I II III
BABY, I'M WINTERTIME COLD I II
By **Meesha**

A GANGSTER'S CODE I &, II III
A GANGSTER'S SYN I II III
THE SAVAGE LIFE I II III
CHAINED TO THE STREETS I II III
BLOOD ON THE MONEY I II III
A GANGSTA'S PAIN I II III
By **J-Blunt**

PUSH IT TO THE LIMIT
By **Bre' Hayes**

BLOOD OF A BOSS I, II, III, IV, V
SHADOWS OF THE GAME
TRAP BASTARD
By **Askari**

THE STREETS BLEED MURDER I, II & III
THE HEART OF A GANGSTA I II& III
By **Jerry Jackson**

CUM FOR ME I II III IV V VI VII VIII
An **LDP Erotica Collaboration**

BRIDE OF A HUSTLA I II & II
THE FETTI GIRLS I, II& III
CORRUPTED BY A GANGSTA I, II III, IV
BLINDED BY HIS LOVE
THE PRICE YOU PAY FOR LOVE I, II ,III
DOPE GIRL MAGIC I II III
By **Destiny Skai**

WHEN A GOOD GIRL GOES BAD
By **Adrienne**

A GANGSTER'S REVENGE I II III & IV
THE BOSS MAN'S DAUGHTERS I II III IV V
A SAVAGE LOVE I & II
BAE BELONGS TO ME I II
A HUSTLER'S DECEIT I, II, III
WHAT BAD BITCHES DO I, II, III
SOUL OF A MONSTER I II III
KILL ZONE
A DOPE BOY'S QUEEN I II III
TIL DEATH
By **Aryanna**

THE COST OF LOYALTY I II III
By Kweli

A KINGPIN'S AMBITION
A KINGPIN'S AMBITION **II**
I MURDER FOR THE DOUGH
By **Ambitious**

TRUE SAVAGE I II III IV V VI VII
DOPE BOY MAGIC I, II, III
MIDNIGHT CARTEL I II III
CITY OF KINGZ I II
NIGHTMARE ON SILENT AVE
THE PLUG OF LIL MEXICO II
CLASSIC CITY
By **Chris Green**

A DOPEBOY'S PRAYER
By **Eddie "Wolf" Lee**

THE KING CARTEL I, II & III
By **Frank Gresham**

THESE NIGGAS AIN'T LOYAL I, II & III
By **Nikki Tee**

GANGSTA SHYT I II &III
By **CATO**

THE ULTIMATE BETRAYAL
By **Phoenix**

BOSS'N UP I, II & III
By **Royal Nicole**

STEPPERS | KING RIO

I LOVE YOU TO DEATH
By **Destiny J**

I RIDE FOR MY HITTA
I STILL RIDE FOR MY HITTA
By **Misty Holt**

LOVE & CHASIN' PAPER
By **Qay Crockett**

TO DIE IN VAIN
SINS OF A HUSTLA
By **ASAD**

BROOKLYN HUSTLAZ
By **Boogsy Morina**

BROOKLYN ON LOCK I & II
By **Sonovia**

GANGSTA CITY
By **Teddy Duke**

A DRUG KING AND HIS DIAMOND I & II III
A DOPEMAN'S RICHES
HER MAN, MINE'S TOO I, II
CASH MONEY HO'S
THE WIFEY I USED TO BE I II
PRETTY GIRLS DO NASTY THINGS
By Nicole Goosby

LIPSTICK KILLAH I, II, III
CRIME OF PASSION I II & III
FRIEND OR FOE I II III
By **Mimi**

TRAPHOUSE KING I II & III
KINGPIN KILLAZ I II III
STREET KINGS I II
PAID IN BLOOD I II
CARTEL KILLAZ I II III
DOPE GODS I II
By **Hood Rich**

STEADY MOBBN' I, II, III
THE STREETS STAINED MY SOUL I II III
By **Marcellus Allen**

WHO SHOT YA I, II, III
SON OF A DOPE FIEND I II
HEAVEN GOT A GHETTO I II
SKI MASK MONEY I II
By **Renta**

GORILLAZ IN THE BAY I II III IV
TEARS OF A GANGSTA I II
3X KRAZY I II
STRAIGHT BEAST MODE I II
By **DE'KARI**

TRIGGADALE I II III
MURDA WAS THE CASE I II
By **Elijah R. Freeman**

THE STREETS ARE CALLING
By **Duquie Wilson**

SLAUGHTER GANG I II III
RUTHLESS HEART I II III
By **Willie Slaughter**

STEPPERS | KING RIO

GOD BLESS THE TRAPPERS I, II, III
THESE SCANDALOUS STREETS I, II, III
FEAR MY GANGSTA I, II, III IV, V
THESE STREETS DON'T LOVE NOBODY I, II
BURY ME A G I, II, III, IV, V
A GANGSTA'S EMPIRE I, II, III, IV
THE DOPEMAN'S BODYGAURD I II
THE REALEST KILLAZ I II III
THE LAST OF THE OGS I II III
By **Tranay Adams**

MARRIED TO A BOSS I II III
By **Destiny Skai & Chris Green**

KINGZ OF THE GAME I II III IV V VI VII
CRIME BOSS
By **Playa Ray**

FUK SHYT
By **Blakk Diamond**

DON'T F#CK WITH MY HEART I II
By **Linnea**

ADDICTED TO THE DRAMA I II III
IN THE ARM OF HIS BOSS II
By **Jamila**

YAYO I II III IV
A SHOOTER'S AMBITION I II
BRED IN THE GAME
By **S. Allen**

LOYALTY AIN'T PROMISED I II
By **Keith Williams**

TRAP GOD I II III
RICH $AVAGE I II III
MONEY IN THE GRAVE I II III
By **Martell Troublesome Bolden**

FOREVER GANGSTA I II
GLOCKS ON SATIN SHEETS I II
By **Adrian Dulan**

TOE TAGZ I II III IV
LEVELS TO THIS SHYT I II
IT'S JUST ME AND YOU
By **Ah'Million**

KINGPIN DREAMS I II III
RAN OFF ON DA PLUG
By **Paper Boi Rari**

CONFESSIONS OF A GANGSTA I II III IV
CONFESSIONS OF A JACKBOY I II
By **Nicholas Lock**

I'M NOTHING WITHOUT HIS LOVE
SINS OF A THUG
TO THE THUG I LOVED BEFORE
A GANGSTA SAVED XMAS
IN A HUSTLER I TRUST
By **Monet Dragun**

QUIET MONEY I II III
THUG LIFE I II III
EXTENDED CLIP I II
A GANGSTA'S PARADISE
By **Trai'Quan**

STEPPERS | KING RIO

CAUGHT UP IN THE LIFE I II III
THE STREETS NEVER LET GO I II III
By **Robert Baptiste**

NEW TO THE GAME I II III
MONEY, MURDER & MEMORIES I II III
By **Malik D. Rice**

CREAM I II III
THE STREETS WILL TALK
By **Yolanda Moore**

LIFE OF A SAVAGE I II III IV
A GANGSTA'S QUR'AN I II III IV
MURDA SEASON I II III
GANGLAND CARTEL I II III
CHI'RAQ GANGSTAS I II III IV
KILLERS ON ELM STREET I II III
JACK BOYZ N DA BRONX I II III
A DOPEBOY'S DREAM I II III
JACK BOYS VS DOPE BOYS I II III
COKE GIRLZ
COKE BOYS
SOSA GANG I II
BRONX SAVAGES
BODYMORE KINGPINS
By **Romell Tukes**

THE STREETS MADE ME I II III
By **Larry D. Wright**

CONCRETE KILLA I II III
VICIOUS LOYALTY I II III
By **Kingpen**

THE ULTIMATE SACRIFICE I, II, III, IV, V, VI
KHADIFI
IF YOU CROSS ME ONCE I II
ANGEL I II III IV
IN THE BLINK OF AN EYE
By **Anthony Fields**

THE LIFE OF A HOOD STAR
By **Ca$h & Rashia Wilson**

THE STREETS WILL NEVER CLOSE I II III
By **K'ajji**

NIGHTMARES OF A HUSTLA I II III
By **King Dream**

HARD AND RUTHLESS I II
MOB TOWN 251
THE BILLIONAIRE BENTLEYS I II III
REAL G'S MOVE IN SILENCE
By **Von Diesel**

GHOST MOB
By **Stilloan Robinson**

MOB TIES I II III IV V VI
SOUL OF A HUSTLER, HEART OF A KILLER I II
GORILLAZ IN THE TRENCHES
By **SayNoMore**

BODYMORE MURDERLAND I II III
THE BIRTH OF A GANGSTER I II
By **Delmont Player**

STEPPERS | KING RIO

FOR THE LOVE OF A BOSS
By **C. D. Blue**

KILLA KOUNTY I II III IV
By Khufu

MOBBED UP I II III IV
THE BRICK MAN I II III IV V
THE COCAINE PRINCESS I II III IV V VI VII
By **King Rio**

MONEY GAME I II
By **Smoove Dolla**

A GANGSTA'S KARMA I II III
By **FLAME**

KING OF THE TRENCHES I II III
By **GHOST & TRANAY ADAMS**

QUEEN OF THE ZOO I II
By **Black Migo**

GRIMEY WAYS I II III
By **Ray Vinci**

XMAS WITH AN ATL SHOOTER
By **Ca$h & Destiny Skai**

KING KILLA
By **Vincent "Vitto" Holloway**

BETRAYAL OF A THUG I II
By **Fre$h**

STEPPERS | KING RIO

THE MURDER QUEENS I II
By **Michael Gallon**

TREAL LOVE
By **Le'Monica Jackson**

FOR THE LOVE OF BLOOD I II
By **Jamel Mitchell**

HOOD CONSIGLIERE I II
By **Keese**

PROTÉGÉ OF A LEGEND I II
LOVE IN THE TRENCHES
By **Corey Robinson**

BORN IN THE GRAVE I II III
By **Self Made Tay**

MOAN IN MY MOUTH
By **XTASY**

TORN BETWEEN A GANGSTER AND A
GENTLEMAN
By **J-BLUNT & Miss Kim**

LOYALTY IS EVERYTHING I II
By **Molotti**

HERE TODAY GONE TOMORROW
By **Fly Rock**

PILLOW PRINCESS
By **S. Hawkins**

BOOKS BY LDP'S CEO, CA$H

TRUST IN NO MAN
TRUST IN NO MAN 2
TRUST IN NO MAN 3
BONDED BY BLOOD
SHORTY GOT A THUG
THUGS CRY
THUGS CRY 2
THUGS CRY 3
TRUST NO BITCH
TRUST NO BITCH 2
TRUST NO BITCH 3
TIL MY CASKET DROPS
RESTRAINING ORDER
RESTRAINING ORDER 2
IN LOVE WITH A CONVICT
LIFE OF A HOOD STAR
XMAS WITH AN ATL SHOOTER

www.ingramcontent.com/pod-product-compliance
Lightning Source LLC
Chambersburg PA
CBHW070455260626
47161CB00004B/1319